THE HEAVY BROW OF HAKALD FAIRHAIR

HILMARJ TORGRIM

MANDOLIN PUBLISHING
Published by the Mandolin Publishing Group

CHAPTER 1:
Roots of a Kingdom

The year was 849 AD, in the cold and unforgiving hills of southeastern Norway. The fjords, dark and deep, cut into the land like the fingers of giants, their jagged edges mirrored by the towering mountains that loomed over the small wooden homes scattered along the coast. Life here was as harsh as the wind that whipped across the seas, a life forged by necessity and survival. But amidst this rugged landscape, something new was stirring, something destined to change the course of the northern world. This was the world into which Harald, the future Fairhair, would be born—but first, there was his family.

Halfdan the Black was already a king, though by modern standards, his title held little meaning beyond his personal holdings. His realm, the small kingdom of Vestfold, was just one of many petty kingdoms that dotted the landscape of Norway. It wasn't wealth or power that distinguished Halfdan; it was his lineage. He came from a long line of kings, stretching back to the mythical Ynglings, said to be descended from the gods themselves. To his people, this heritage meant something—though it would be his son, not Halfdan, who would make it matter on a grander scale.

Halfdan ruled with the strength of his sword and the loyalty of his warriors, a balance carefully maintained through gifts of land, promises of raids, and the forging of alliances. The political climate of Norway at the time was one of constant tension. Kings rose and fell as quickly as the tides; alliances were made over mead only to be broken at the first sign of weakness. Vestfold, nestled along the Oslofjord, was strategically important, a kingdom of trade routes and fertile land, always vulnerable to invasion or rebellion. Yet Halfdan had managed to hold his realm together through both cunning and force, expanding his influence over neighboring regions and consolidating power in the southern part of Norway.

The people of Vestfold were as tough as the land they inhabited. Fishermen and farmers by necessity, warriors by tradition, they lived in a society where survival was often a matter of how well one could swing an axe or how sharp one's spear was. The long winters, filled with cold and darkness, bred a hardy folk, accustomed to hardship and unafraid of death. Honor and loyalty were paramount; to be a warrior was to embrace the risk of dying in battle, which, to the Norse mind, meant a chance at eternal life in Valhalla. These values were ingrained in every household, from the lowest freeman to the king himself.

Inside Halfdan's hall, though, there was an unusual air of anticipation. His wife, Ragnhild, had come to him from a neighboring kingdom, an alliance sealed with marriage as so many were. She was renowned for her beauty and wisdom, though in truth, it was her political connections that had made her most valuable to Halfdan. She was carrying his heir, and though Halfdan already had several sons from other marriages, Ragnhild's child was expected to be different. The gods had already whispered of great things to come from this boy, or so the seers claimed.

In those days, the birth of a child—especially the son of a king—was more than a simple matter of family. It was a political event, one that could shift the balance of power in a region. Ragnhild, despite the uncomfortable weight of her pregnancy, still played a key role in the affairs of the kingdom, advising Halfdan on matters of diplomacy and the ever-shifting alliances between Norway's many small, warring factions. She was no mere queen in the background; she was an active player in Halfdan's plans for expansion. And she understood that the birth of this child would cement her own status, and by extension, the future of the kingdom.

As the months passed, Halfdan continued to build his power, sending emissaries to neighboring kings and expanding his influence through calculated marriages and alliances. Word of the growing strength of Vestfold spread, and with it came both envy and fear. The smaller kings, who ruled over territories of no more than a few dozen farms, watched Halfdan warily. Some sought his favor, while others plotted in secret to undermine him. The fractured nature of Norway, with its patchwork of feuding chieftains and kings, meant that power was fragile, and everyone knew it.

It was into this world of conflict and ambition that Harald would be born. The child, the seers said, would grow to be greater than any king before him, a man destined to unite the fractured lands of Norway under one crown. The prophecy hung over Halfdan's hall like a shadow, a promise of glory but also a reminder of the blood that would be shed to achieve it.

In the spring of 850, as the ice began to melt and the days grew longer, Ragnhild's time came. The entire kingdom seemed to hold its breath. Inside the longhouse, the air was thick with the smell of burning wood and herbs, meant to keep the spirits at bay. The midwives, skilled in the ancient ways, moved quietly around the room as Ragnhild labored, her cries echoing against the wooden beams of the hall. Halfdan, like any man of his station, waited outside, pacing restlessly but never daring to enter the room. This was a moment for women and gods, not for men.

After hours that stretched into an eternity, the wail of a newborn broke the tension. A son was born. Harald. His arrival was met with both relief and expectation, as the seers whispered of the greatness that awaited him. Halfdan, upon hearing the news, stepped into the room for the first time. There, amid the low light of flickering fires, he gazed upon his newborn son. The child was strong, the midwives said, with the thick dark hair of his father. But more than that, there was a sense—unspoken but present—that this boy was different. His birth marked the beginning of something greater than the petty conflicts of neighboring kings.

Halfdan bent down to take his son in his arms, his face hard but his heart swelling with a rare emotion he did not often allow himself to feel—hope. He had conquered much, but this child, this tiny bundle in his hands, was his greatest conquest yet. He would shape the boy into the man the seers promised, a man destined to reshape the world around him. The road ahead would be long and bloody, but Halfdan had no doubt that his son was the one who would fulfill the prophecy and unite the kingdoms.

In the years to come, that prophecy would set Harald on a path of war, ambition, and unyielding determination. But for now, as the cold winds of Norway swept over the land, the future king slept soundly in his father's arms, unaware of the weight of destiny that lay upon him.

Chapter 2
The Boy Who Would be King

Harald's early years were shaped by the rough hands of fate and the sharpened edges of a world constantly on the brink of war. As the son of Halfdan the Black, a king who commanded both respect and fear in equal measure, Harald grew up surrounded by the constant murmur of politics, the clash of steel, and the ever-present awareness that the world was not a place for the weak. His father's halls echoed with the stories of bloodshed and conquest, and from the moment Harald could understand speech, he was taught that his life would be no different.

The boy grew quickly, strong for his age, and sharp-eyed. From the time he could walk, Harald was treated not simply as the king's son, but as a future warrior, a chieftain, and a man whose destiny lay far beyond the borders of Vestfold. His upbringing was not one of indulgence. The luxury one might imagine for a prince was almost nonexistent in the cold, wind-bitten halls of his father. Instead, Harald's days were filled with hard lessons—hunting in the dense forests that bordered the fjords, wrestling with boys older than himself, and learning the way of the sword and axe from the hardened warriors in his father's service.

The harsh conditions of Norway shaped Harald, just as they shaped every other boy who lived through them. Life in the north was not forgiving. Winters stretched long and cruel, and when the summer sun finally returned, it was often met with the violence of raids and conflicts between rival kingdoms. Yet, these early challenges honed Harald in ways that could not be taught in any royal court. The jagged cliffs, icy waters, and dense forests of Norway became as much his teachers as his tutors and warriors. He learned to read the sky, to track game through the underbrush, and to wield a blade as though it were an extension of his own arm.

By the age of ten, Harald was already the image of his father. Broad-shouldered, with the beginnings of what would one day become the famous Fairhair, he carried himself with a sense of quiet authority. While other boys still squabbled over games and sought the approval of their elders, Harald had a deeper, more serious look in his eyes. He understood, on some level, that his life would not follow the same path as the children of lesser men. His destiny was laid out before him, and even at such a young age, he began to sense the weight of the crown that one day would rest upon his head.

As Harald grew, Halfdan the Black continued to consolidate his power. His father's conquests became more frequent and ambitious, spreading his influence deeper into Norway. Every victory added to the legend of the Yngling line and secured more resources and allies. Harald watched and listened, absorbing the strategies and alliances that shaped his father's reign. He learned not only the art of war but also the delicate balance of politics. His father was no fool—Halfdan knew that a king's power did not lie solely in his sword. It was in the ability to manipulate others, to see opportunities in enemies and danger in allies.

It was around this time that Harald's training took on a more formal aspect. He began to ride out with his father's men, joining them on hunting trips that doubled as lessons in warfare. These hunts, though ostensibly peaceful, were never far from the shadow of violence. Rival chieftains prowled the borders of Halfdan's territory, and skirmishes could break out at any moment. On more than one occasion, Harald found himself in the midst of a brawl, fending off attackers with nothing more than a sharpened stick or the hilt of a short sword. Though these encounters were not battles in the true sense, they were lessons in survival, and Harald proved himself quick to learn.

By the time he turned twelve, Harald had killed his first man. It was during one of these hunts, when a group of raiders from a neighboring kingdom ambushed them on the edge of a forest. The air was thick with the scent of pine and blood as the clash of swords rang through the trees. Harald, thrust into the chaos, fought as he had been taught—without fear, without hesitation. In the end, he stood over the body of a man twice his age, bloodied and breathless, but victorious. It was a rite of passage, one that left an indelible mark on him. He had stepped into manhood not through ceremony, but through the harsh, cold reality of the axe.

That night, as the men feasted and drank in celebration, Halfdan approached his son. Harald was still shaken by the violence, the memory of the man's last breath playing over in his mind. But his father's gaze was steady, a mixture of pride and something else—something harder, more calculating.

"Remember this," Halfdan had said, his voice low and rough. "A king must always be ready to kill. But more than that, a king must know why he kills."

It was a lesson that would stay with Harald for the rest of his life.

As the years passed, Harald's reputation grew. His strength and courage became known throughout Vestfold and beyond. By the time he was fourteen, he was already a leader among the younger warriors, commanding respect with a natural authority that belied his youth. His father's men spoke of him in hushed tones, predicting greatness for the boy who had the blood of the Ynglings in his veins.

Yet, despite his growing prowess, Harald was still a boy in many ways. He listened to the stories of his ancestors with wide eyes, fascinated by the tales of gods and heroes who had walked the earth before him. The sagas, filled with accounts of Odin, Thor, and the great battles of the past, fueled his imagination and filled him with a sense of purpose. He began to believe that his destiny was not merely to rule Vestfold, but to unite all of Norway. The thought both excited and terrified him. To bring together the fractured kingdoms of Norway under one banner was a task that no man had ever achieved, but Harald could feel the weight of it pressing down on him, urging him forward.

As Harald grew into manhood, the responsibilities of his future began to take shape. His father, aging but still formidable, started to involve him in matters of state. Harald attended councils, listened to the disputes between neighboring chieftains, and began to understand the delicate dance of alliances and betrayals that held the kingdom together. He watched as his father negotiated peace with one hand while preparing for war with the other. It was a dangerous game, one that Harald knew he would one day have to master.

Chapter 3
Harald Finds Girls

Harald was sixteen when he first felt the unfamiliar pull of something that had nothing to do with swords, power, or politics. The fields outside the village of Borre, where his father's seat lay, stretched wide and golden in the short summer months, the wildflowers blooming in defiance of the harsh winters that had left their mark on the land. It was on one of these days, as Harald rode along the outskirts of the village, that he noticed her for the first time.

She was different from the other girls of the village. Most of them stayed close to their families, tending to the daily work of the household—minding the sheep, weaving, or preparing food for the winter to come. But this girl moved with an ease that was unusual. She was tall and strong, with a wild mane of dark hair that caught the wind, and eyes that seemed to spark with life even when she wasn't smiling. She was helping her brothers repair a wooden fence when Harald's eyes fell on her, and something inside him shifted.

He hadn't known her before—she must have come from one of the outlying farms that had recently allied with his father's kingdom. In the years since Halfdan had expanded his influence, more families had come to settle under his protection, bringing with them new faces and new loyalties. But this girl didn't seem interested in politics. As he passed by on his horse, she looked up briefly, her eyes meeting his for just a moment before she turned back to her work, completely unfazed by the sight of the king's son.

That brief glance stayed with him for days. It was the first time Harald had been caught off guard by someone who wasn't a rival warrior or a battlefield opponent. His life until now had been singular in its focus—preparing for the day when he would take his father's place as ruler of Vestfold, and perhaps even more. There had been little time, or inclination, for the distractions of youth. But something about the girl stirred something unfamiliar in him, something he couldn't quite name but that filled his mind whenever he was not at the training grounds or in council with his father.

He didn't know her name. For all his strength and boldness, Harald found himself strangely uncertain of how to approach her. It wasn't fear—he had faced death and spilled blood, but this was different. This was a subtle vulnerability he hadn't encountered before. The next time he saw her, she was walking with a basket of wild herbs through the woods, her stride confident and unhurried, as if the world moved at her pace and not the other way around. Harald, watching from a distance, wondered what it would be like to speak to her, to break the silence that had so far defined their encounters.

It took him another week before he finally mustered the courage to approach her. The chance came when he was out riding alone, taking a break from the politics of his father's court. He spotted her by the river, her skirts hitched up as she stood knee-deep in the water, gathering reeds. He reined in his horse and dismounted, telling himself that it was just curiosity, nothing more. He was a king's son, after all. What did it matter what one village girl thought of him?

She didn't notice him at first, her focus entirely on her task. Harald walked toward her, the tall grass crunching underfoot, until she finally looked up. Her eyes flashed in the sunlight, sharp and clear, and there was no surprise on her face—just a calm, measured acknowledgment of his presence. She straightened, wiping her hands on her skirts before meeting his gaze head-on.

"You're Harald," she said simply, as though stating a fact, not offering deference.

Harald felt a strange mixture of embarrassment and amusement. "I am," he replied, a half-smile tugging at the corner of his mouth. "And you are?"

"Gry," she answered, glancing at his horse before looking back at him. "What brings the future king to this part of the village?"

Her tone was casual, as if she were speaking to any other boy, and it caught Harald off guard. He was used to people—especially villagers—treating him with a mix of reverence and fear. But Gry seemed unimpressed by his title, and for reasons he couldn't explain, that only made him more intrigued.

"I was riding," Harald said, shifting slightly as he tried to think of something to say that didn't sound foolish. "And I saw you. Thought I'd say hello."

Gry raised an eyebrow, her lips quirking into a wry smile. "Did you now?"

Harald wasn't sure what to make of her. She was bold, almost insolent, but in a way that didn't feel disrespectful. It was refreshing, if a little unsettling. He found himself at a loss for words, something that rarely happened to him. The tension between them hung in the air for a moment, and then Gry turned back to her reeds, her fingers deftly weaving them into a small basket.

"I've seen you around," she said after a pause, her tone softer now, as though offering an olive branch. "You're always busy. Preparing for war, I suppose."

Harald nodded, though he wasn't sure how much of it was true. "That's part of it," he admitted, watching her work. "But there's more to it. My father wants to unite the kingdoms. That means a lot of alliances, a lot of diplomacy. It's not all about fighting."

Gry looked up at him again, her expression thoughtful. "Is that what you want?" she asked, her voice curious rather than challenging.

Harald hesitated. No one had ever asked him that before. His life had always been defined by what was expected of him, by the weight of his father's ambitions and the legacy of the Ynglings. But in that moment, standing by the river with Gry, he felt a flicker of something different—something that made him question, for the first time, whether his path was as set in stone as he had always believed.

"I don't know," he admitted quietly, surprised by his own honesty.

For a moment, neither of them spoke. The only sound was the soft rush of the river and the distant call of birds. Then Gry smiled, a real one this time, and it lit up her face in a way that made Harald's chest tighten.

"Well," she said, standing up and dusting off her skirts, "when you figure it out, let me know."

With that, she gathered her basket and walked past him, leaving Harald standing by the river, more confused than ever. But as he watched her disappear into the trees, he knew one thing for certain—he would be seeing more of Gry. And that thought, strange as it was, made him feel lighter than he had in a long time.

Chapter 4
Love in the
Shadows

The days following his encounter with Gry were marked by a new kind of restlessness in Harald. He had faced countless challenges in his young life—brutal winters, fierce battles, the ever-present expectations of his father—but none of them had unsettled him the way she did. It wasn't just the casual way she had spoken to him, as though he were no different from the other boys in the village. It was the fact that she seemed to see something in him that no one else did—something beyond the future king, the warrior, the son of Halfdan the Black.

Harald found himself looking for excuses to visit the village more often, though he would never have admitted it to anyone. He took to riding alone, leaving behind the hustle of court and the prying eyes of his father's warriors. There was a freedom in those solitary rides, a brief escape from the weight of his responsibilities. But more than that, they were a chance to see Gry again.

Weeks passed before their paths crossed a second time. This time, it was at the village market, where traders from nearby settlements had gathered to exchange goods before the first snows. The square was bustling with activity—children darted between stalls, women haggled over the price of wool, and the scent of roasted meat filled the air. Harald kept to the edge of the crowd, his hood pulled low over his face to avoid attracting attention. He wasn't sure what he was looking for, but when he spotted Gry, his heart leaped in his chest.

She was standing near one of the stalls, talking animatedly with an older woman—her mother, perhaps? Harald couldn't be sure. From a distance, she looked much the same as she had by the river—confident, with that same wild spark in her eyes. But there was something else about her now, something that made Harald feel both drawn to her and unsure of how to approach her again.

He waited until she was alone, walking toward the edge of the market with a basket of fresh bread in her hands. Stepping out of the shadows, Harald fell into step beside her, trying to ignore the quickening of his pulse.

"Gry," he said, his voice quieter than usual.

She glanced at him, her eyes widening slightly in surprise before a small smile curved her lips. "Harald," she replied, her tone teasing. "Hiding from the crowd, are you?"

"Something like that," Harald admitted, his lips twitching into a grin despite himself. "Too many eyes."

They walked in silence for a few moments, the noise of the market fading behind them as they reached the quieter part of the village. The air was crisp, the autumn chill settling in as the last of the summer warmth disappeared. Gry's presence beside him was both comforting and unnerving, her easy confidence a stark contrast to the uncertainty swirling in his chest.

"You're not like the others," Gry said suddenly, breaking the silence. She wasn't looking at him, but at the path ahead, her voice thoughtful. "The other men in your father's court, I mean. They're all so sure of themselves. So focused on power, on what's expected of them. But you..." She trailed off, finally turning to meet his gaze. "You seem different."

Harald frowned, not sure how to respond. He had spent his entire life preparing for a role that had been set for him since birth. To hear someone suggest that he might not be as fixed in that path as he thought—it stirred something inside him that he wasn't ready to confront.

"I'm not sure that's a good thing," he said, his voice low.

Gry stopped walking, turning to face him fully now. "Who said it wasn't?" she asked, her eyes searching his face.

For a moment, they stood there, the village quiet around them. Harald felt the pull between them more strongly than ever, a strange and powerful force that both excited and terrified him. He had never allowed himself to feel anything like this before. His life had always been about strength, discipline, and control. But Gry—she made him want something else, something he couldn't name.

Before he could think better of it, Harald reached out, his fingers brushing hers where she held the basket. Gry didn't pull away. Instead, she met his gaze with that same boldness, her lips curving into a small, knowing smile.

"You don't have to be what they expect," she said quietly. "You can be whoever you want to be."

Harald swallowed, his throat suddenly tight. It was as if Gry had spoken aloud the thoughts he had been trying to bury, the doubts and questions that had gnawed at him since he was old enough to understand what being a king's son truly meant. For the first time, he felt like he wasn't alone in his uncertainty.   Someone   understood—Gry understood.

"I don't know if I can," Harald said, his voice barely above a whisper.

Gry's smile softened, and she squeezed his hand gently before pulling away. "You'll figure it out," she said, her tone light again, though her eyes remained serious. "I have faith in you."

Harald watched her walk away, disappearing into the narrow streets of the village. He stood there long after she was gone, the weight of her words lingering in the crisp autumn air.

That night, as he lay in his bed, staring up at the wooden beams of his father's hall, Harald thought of Gry's smile, her words echoing in his mind. It was the first time anyone had ever challenged him to think beyond the crown, beyond the expectations that had been laid upon him since birth. And though he knew he couldn't escape his destiny, a small part of him wondered—just for a moment—what his life might look like if he followed a different path. If he allowed himself to want something for himself, rather than for his father, for Vestfold, for Norway.

But such thoughts were dangerous, and Harald knew it. His life was not his own to shape. Not yet.

For now, Gry would remain the one thing in his life that was truly his—his secret, his hidden flame in the shadows of duty and ambition. And though he couldn't act on the feelings that stirred within him, he knew that they would never truly leave him.

Chapter 5
The Weight of Destiny

The morning sun filtered through the thin wooden shutters of Harald's chamber, casting faint patterns of light across the floor. He had slept fitfully, his dreams restless and filled with fleeting images of Gry—her dark hair caught in the wind, her eyes piercing through his doubts. As much as he tried to shake the thoughts of her, they lingered in the back of his mind, a quiet rebellion against the path his life was supposed to follow.

Outside, the sounds of daily life at his father's court were already stirring. The clang of metal echoed from the training grounds, where warriors sparred under the watchful eyes of their commanders. In the great hall, the kitchen servants were busy preparing the morning meal, and Harald could hear his father's deep voice carrying over the din of conversation. Halfdan the Black, ruler of Vestfold, was a man of towering presence, both in stature and reputation. His ambitions were as vast as the lands he sought to conquer, and Harald had always known that it was his destiny to carry those ambitions forward.

But now, the weight of that destiny felt heavier than ever.

Harald dressed quickly, pulling on his tunic and fastening his belt before heading out into the courtyard. He needed air, space to think—anything to clear his mind of the turmoil that had taken root there. The crisp autumn breeze hit him as he stepped outside, the chill of the approaching winter already seeping into the air. Around him, the warriors of Vestfold moved with purpose, some preparing for patrols, others discussing tactics and strategies for the upcoming raids.

Harald's mind, however, was elsewhere.

As he made his way toward the stables, his father's voice called out from behind him. He turned to see Halfdan striding toward him, his brow furrowed with the intensity that was never far from his face.

"Harald," Halfdan said, clapping a hand on his son's shoulder. "I've been looking for you. There is much to discuss."

Harald nodded, though his thoughts remained distant. "What is it, Father?"

Halfdan's grip tightened slightly, his eyes narrowing. "The time has come to take a more active role in our expansion. You're nearly a man now, and it's time you learned what it truly means to rule. There are lands to be claimed, alliances to be forged—and battles to be fought."

Harald stiffened. He had known this conversation was coming, but hearing it spoken aloud made the burden all the more real. For years, he had trained with the finest warriors, honing his skills with sword and spear, preparing for the day when he would take his father's place. But now, with his mind clouded by thoughts of Gry and the doubts she had stirred, the idea of leading men into battle felt suddenly more daunting.

"I understand," Harald said, trying to mask the unease in his voice.

Halfdan eyed him closely, as if sensing the hesitation. "Do you?" he asked, his tone sharp. "This is not a game, Harald. The kingdoms of Norway are divided, and the only way to unite them is through strength—our strength. If we don't seize the opportunity, someone else will. You were born for this."

Harald nodded, though the words rang hollow in his ears. He had been told his entire life that he was born for this, that his destiny was to rule and to conquer. But standing there, under the weight of his father's expectations, he couldn't help but wonder if that was all there was to it.

"I'm ready," Harald said finally, forcing the words out.

Halfdan's expression softened slightly, though the intensity in his eyes remained. "Good," he said. "You'll ride with me in a week's time. There's a small kingdom to the north—petty and weak, but strategically valuable. We'll take it by force if necessary, and you'll lead the charge. It's time for the people to see you as more than just my son."

Harald swallowed hard, the reality of what his father was asking sinking in. Leading the charge meant more than just swinging a sword. It meant taking lives, commanding men, and carrying the weight of every decision on his shoulders. It was the role he had been preparing for his entire life, but now, standing on the edge of that reality, it felt impossibly vast.

"I won't disappoint you," Harald said, though a small voice inside him wondered if that was the truth.

Halfdan clapped him on the shoulder again, his grip firm. "I know you won't. You're my son—my blood. And soon, the rest of Norway will know it too."

With that, Halfdan turned and strode away, leaving Harald standing alone in the courtyard. The wind picked up, tugging at his tunic as he watched his father disappear into the great hall. For a moment, he stood there, his mind racing with thoughts of the impending raid, the expectations placed upon him, and the growing uncertainty gnawing at his resolve.

Without thinking, his feet carried him toward the stables, where his horse waited. He needed to clear his head, and there was only one place he could think to go.

The village was quieter than usual when Harald arrived, his horse's hooves kicking up dust as he rode through the narrow streets. He had no real plan, no excuse for coming here again, but the thought of seeing Gry—of talking to her, if only for a moment—had drawn him in like a lodestone. She had a way of cutting through the noise, of making everything feel simpler, if only for a brief time.

He found her in the fields, as he had before, her dark hair pulled back from her face as she worked alongside her brothers, gathering what was left of the late autumn harvest. She didn't notice him at first, her focus entirely on the task at hand. But

33

when she did look up, her eyes locked onto his, and a small smile curved her lips.

"You're back," she said, her tone teasing as she straightened up. "I didn't expect to see you again so soon."

Harald dismounted, his heart pounding in his chest for reasons he couldn't fully explain. "I needed to get away," he admitted, his voice quieter than usual.

Gry's smile faded slightly, and she studied him with a seriousness that made him feel exposed, as though she could see straight through the walls he had built around himself.

"What's weighing on you?" she asked, her voice soft but direct.

Harald hesitated, unsure of how to put his thoughts into words. He had never been one to confide in others—especially not about his doubts. But there was something about Gry that made him want to speak the truth, even if it was uncomfortable.

"My father wants me to lead a raid," he said finally, his gaze dropping to the ground. "It's what I've been trained for, what I'm supposed to do. But…"

"But you're not sure you want it," Gry finished for him, her voice quiet but steady.

Harald looked up at her, surprised by how easily she had understood. He had never voiced these doubts to anyone, and yet here she was, reading his thoughts as though they were written on his face.

"I don't know if I can be what he expects," Harald said, the words coming out before he could stop them.

Gry stepped closer, her eyes searching his. "You don't have to be exactly what he expects," she said gently. "You can lead in your own way. Be the kind of king you want to be, not just the one he wants."

Harald frowned, the weight of her words settling over him like a heavy cloak. He wanted to believe her, wanted to believe that there was another path, one that allowed him to be both a leader and true to himself. But the reality of his situation was far more complicated.

"I don't know if it's that simple," he said, his voice barely above a whisper.

Gry smiled softly, her hand reaching out to brush his arm. "Nothing worth having ever is."

For a moment, they stood there in the fading light of the autumn day, the world around them quiet and still. And though Harald knew that the weight of his destiny still hung heavy over him, Gry's words gave him a glimmer of hope—hope that perhaps, in time, he could find a way to forge his own path, even in the shadow of his father's legacy.

Chapter 6
Rising Tide

The morning of the raid arrived sooner than Harald had anticipated, its cold breath sweeping across the lands of Vestfold. The sky was a deep, bruised gray, thick with clouds that hung low over the fjords, threatening rain or worse. Warriors gathered in the courtyard of his father's longhouse, sharpening their blades, checking their shields, and fastening leather straps around their armor. There was a tense hum in the air, a mixture of anticipation and grim determination. This was the life they had chosen, the life they had been born into.

Harald stood apart from the rest, watching the preparations with a growing sense of unease. His hand rested on the hilt of his sword, a weapon that had been forged specifically for him, its handle engraved with the symbols of his lineage. The blade felt heavy at his side, a reminder of the responsibility he carried—not just for the men who would ride out under his command, but for the future of his father's kingdom.

Halfdan the Black had been clear: this raid was not just a test of Harald's strength, but a declaration to all of Norway that his son was ready to take his place as a leader of men. The small kingdom to the north that they would attack was weak, its ruler old and lacking in the alliances that had kept other regions strong. In theory, it should be an easy victory. But Harald couldn't shake the gnawing doubt in his gut.

"Harald!" his father's voice boomed from the entrance to the hall, cutting through his thoughts. Halfdan strode toward him, his face set in the same determined expression that Harald had come to associate with his father's plans for conquest.

"Are you ready?" Halfdan asked, his eyes sharp as they swept over his son, looking for any sign of weakness.

Harald straightened his shoulders, pushing the doubt aside. "I am."

"Good," Halfdan said, clapping a hand on Harald's shoulder. "Remember, the men will look to you. Lead with strength and confidence, and they will follow."

Harald nodded, though his father's words only added to the weight pressing down on him. He had always known that this day would come, but now that it was here, the reality of it felt suffocating.

As they mounted their horses and rode out of the gates, Harald cast one last glance back toward the village. He knew Gry would not be there to see them off, but the thought of her gave him a small measure of comfort. Her words from the previous day echoed in his mind: *You can lead in your own way.*

The journey to the northern kingdom took them through dense forests and along winding coastal paths. The men were silent for much of the ride, their minds focused on the battle ahead. Harald rode at the front of the column, his father beside him, the two of them flanked by some of Halfdan's most trusted warriors. Though the sky had grown darker, the rain had held off, leaving the ground firm beneath their horses' hooves.

By the time they reached the borders of the northern kingdom, the wind had picked up, howling through the trees like the ghost of some ancient, forgotten god. Harald tightened his grip on the reins, his gaze fixed on the distant hills where the small kingdom's defenses lay. Smoke curled into the sky from the village beyond, a sign that the people there were unaware of the storm that was about to descend upon them.

As the army dismounted and began to prepare for the attack, Halfdan approached Harald, his expression grave. "This is your moment, Harald," he said quietly, his voice carrying only to his son. "Lead them well, and this kingdom will be ours by nightfall."

Harald swallowed, the weight of his father's words settling over him like a heavy cloak. He nodded, his throat tight with the effort of keeping his doubts at bay. This was what he had been trained for, what he had been born to do. But no amount of training could prepare him for the reality of leading men into battle.

The attack began just before dusk, when the fading light would make it harder for the enemy to see their approach. Harald led the charge as planned, his sword drawn and his heart pounding in his chest. The warriors of Vestfold surged forward behind him, their battle cries echoing across the hills as they descended upon the unsuspecting village.

The fighting was fierce but brief. The northern kingdom's defenses crumbled quickly under the onslaught, their warriors outnumbered and unprepared for the brutality of the attack. Harald moved through the chaos with a single-minded focus, his sword flashing as he cut down any who stood in his way. Blood stained the ground beneath him, mixing with the mud and the smoke from the burning village.

By the time the sun had fully set, the battle was over. The northern kingdom had fallen, its ruler slain, and the survivors taken as captives. The warriors of Vestfold stood victorious, their cheers filling the night air as they celebrated their triumph.

Harald stood among them, his chest heaving with the effort of battle, his sword still clutched in his hand. He had led them to victory, just as his father had expected. And yet, as he looked around at the bodies strewn across the ground, at the burning remnants of the village they had destroyed, he couldn't shake the hollow feeling that had taken root inside him.

This was what it meant to be a king. To conquer, to destroy, to take what was not yours by force. It was the path that had been laid out for him, the path he had always known he would walk. But standing there, amid the blood and the smoke, Harald couldn't help but wonder if there was another way.

As the warriors celebrated their victory, Halfdan approached his son, a proud smile on his face. "You did well, Harald," he said, clapping a hand on his shoulder. "The men will speak of this day for years to come."

Harald forced a smile, though the pride he had expected to feel was nowhere to be found. "Thank you, Father," he said quietly.

Halfdan didn't seem to notice his son's unease. He was too caught up in the victory, in the knowledge that his son had proven himself as a leader. "This is only the beginning," Halfdan said, his voice filled with the promise of future conquests. "Soon, all of Norway will know the name of Harald Fairhair."

As the fires burned low and the warriors drank to their victory, Harald slipped away from the celebration, his mind heavy with thoughts of the future. He had done what was expected of him, had proven himself as a leader. But at what cost?

The weight of his father's expectations, of the legacy he was meant to uphold, pressed down on him with every step he took. And for the first time in his life, Harald began to wonder if the path laid out before him was truly the one he wanted to walk.

The wind howled through the trees as Harald stood alone on the edge of the battlefield, the distant sounds of celebration fading into the night. He stared out at the darkened horizon, his thoughts a storm of doubt and uncertainty.

In the distance, the sea stretched out endlessly, its waves crashing against the rocky shore with a force that mirrored the turmoil inside him. Harald had always been taught that strength was the only way to rule, that power came from the sword and the crown. But now, standing on the cusp of a future that seemed both inevitable and unbearable, he couldn't help but wonder if there was another way.

And in the quiet of the night, Harald made a silent vow to himself: that no matter what lay ahead, he would find a way to be more than just the warrior his father wanted him to be. He would find a way to be the man—and the leader—that he wanted to be.

Even if it meant walking a path no one else could see.

Chapter 7
Weight of Victory

Harald sat on a ridge overlooking the village, the remnants of the battle still smoldering below him. From this vantage, he could see the burnt-out houses, the scattered bodies, the prisoners herded into a makeshift camp. His men celebrated their triumph, voices raised in songs of glory and victory, but Harald found no joy in it. He felt only the weight of the bloodshed, the destruction they had wrought.

The night had grown cold, the crisp autumn air biting at his skin as he wrapped his cloak tighter around his shoulders. The stars hung low in the sky, their light dim and distant. It should have been a night of triumph, a night to revel in his success as a leader. Instead, it felt hollow.

A soft crunch of footsteps approached from behind, and Harald turned to see one of his father's warriors, a man named Sigurd, standing at a respectful distance. Sigurd was older, with deep lines etched into his face from years of battle, his hair more silver than blond. He had been a loyal warrior to Halfdan for as long as Harald could remember, always watching, always ready to serve.

"Your father wishes to see you," Sigurd said, his voice low. He glanced at the battlefield below, then back at Harald. "He's with the men."

Harald nodded, standing slowly and brushing the dirt from his cloak. "I'll be there soon."

Sigurd hesitated, then stepped closer. "It's never easy, is it?" he said, his voice softer now. "The first battle. The first victory. You think it'll feel like glory, but it's just blood and smoke."

Harald said nothing, but he appreciated the honesty. Sigurd had seen more battles than he could count, yet the weariness in his voice told Harald that the weight of each one never left him.

"Your father's proud of you," Sigurd continued. "He sees in you the future of Norway. The beginning of something greater than all of us."

Harald looked down at the battlefield once more, his jaw tightening. "I know what he sees."

"And what do you see?" Sigurd asked quietly.

Harald didn't answer. Instead, he nodded to Sigurd and made his way down the ridge. As he approached the camp, the sounds of revelry grew louder, the firelight casting flickering shadows on the faces of the warriors. They drank deeply, laughing, their faces flushed with victory. It was a scene of triumph, but to Harald, it felt distant, like a dream that no longer belonged to him.

His father stood at the center of it all, surrounded by his most trusted men. Halfdan the Black was in his element, his booming laugh cutting through the night as he recounted the day's victory. His presence was larger than life, his voice commanding, his authority unquestionable.

When he saw Harald approach, Halfdan's face broke into a wide grin. "There he is!" he called out, raising a cup of mead in his son's direction. "The man of the hour! Come, Harald, drink with us!"

Harald forced a smile and accepted the cup handed to him, though he barely tasted the bitter mead as it passed his lips. His father clapped him on the back, his voice loud enough for all to hear.

"You led us to victory today, my son," Halfdan said, his eyes gleaming with pride. "This is the first of many battles. Soon, all of Norway will bow to us, and they will remember the name of Harald Fairhair."

The men cheered, raising their cups in salute. Harald nodded, but inside, the unease that had been growing since the battle gnawed at him. He had led them to victory, just as his father had wanted. But something felt wrong.

Later that night, when the fires had died down and the warriors had fallen into a drunken sleep, Harald found himself wandering the outskirts of the camp. The moon hung low in the sky, casting a pale glow over the landscape. He walked in silence, his thoughts heavy.

As he neared the edge of the village, he heard a soft sound—the quiet murmur of voices. Harald paused, straining to hear. It came from one of the surviving houses, a small hut that had somehow escaped the flames. He approached cautiously, his hand resting on the hilt of his sword, though he doubted he would need it.

Inside the hut, a dim light flickered from a dying fire, casting shadows on the walls. Harald peered through the doorway and saw a woman kneeling by the hearth, her back to him. She was speaking softly, her voice soothing, though he couldn't make out the words. In front of her, two small children huddled close together, their faces streaked with dirt and tears.

Harald's chest tightened as he watched them. The woman's voice was steady, though there was an undercurrent of fear in it. She was comforting her children, trying to shield them from the horror of the day. From the violence that had destroyed their home.

He turned away, his heart heavy. This was the price of victory. The lives left in ruin, the innocent caught in the crossfire of ambition and power. He had grown up hearing tales of conquest, of kings who carved their names into history through blood and steel. But standing here, on the edge of this broken village, Harald wondered if those kings had ever felt what he felt now.

The weight of it all—the bloodshed, the loss, the destruction—it pressed down on him like a heavy cloak. He had led his men to victory, but at what cost? Was this truly what it meant to be a king? To leave ruin in his wake?

Harald closed his eyes and took a deep breath, the cool night air filling his lungs. He had made a choice when he rode into battle that morning, a choice to follow the path his father had set for him. But now, as he stood on the edge of that path, he couldn't help but wonder if there was another way. A way that didn't involve burning villages and broken families.

The wind whispered through the trees, carrying with it the scent of the sea. Harald lifted his head and looked out at the horizon, where the dark waves crashed against the distant shore. The sea had always called to him, its vastness a symbol of freedom and possibility. Perhaps there was something to be found out there, beyond the reach of his father's expectations. Something more than blood and conquest.

For now, though, he was bound to this place, to this life. But as Harald turned and made his way back to the camp, a quiet resolve settled over him. He would lead, as his father expected. But he would find his own way to do it.

Chapter 8
The New Alliance

The dawn of a new day brought a hesitant calm to the smoldering remains of the village. The once bustling settlement was now a shadow of its former self, the ruins testifying to the ferocity of Harald's victory. As the sun rose, its light revealed the full extent of the destruction, casting a stark contrast between the bright sky and the charred earth below. Harald, weary and contemplative, awoke to a new reality—one where the cost of conquest was undeniable.

Halfdan, ever the strategist, had already begun the process of consolidating their gains. In the wake of their triumph, the northern kingdom's lands were now under their control, but the true challenge lay in maintaining that control. The few survivors of the village were being rounded up, their fates uncertain. Harald knew that if they were to govern these lands effectively, alliances would need to be formed, and the local leaders needed to be dealt with diplomatically as well as through force.

As Harald joined his father and the council of warriors in the center of their encampment, he saw the tension in the air. The men were exhausted but eager to push forward, their voices a murmur of excited plans and speculation. Halfdan, however, was focused on a different kind of strategy—one that involved diplomacy and alliances rather than further raids.

"We must solidify our hold on this territory," Halfdan declared, his voice commanding attention. "To do so, we need to forge alliances with the neighboring tribes and chieftains. We cannot maintain control through force alone."

Harald listened carefully. His father's plan was clear: they needed to negotiate with the local leaders, establish agreements that would secure their rule, and integrate the newly conquered lands into their expanding realm. The prospect of diplomacy was a new challenge for Harald, one that required a different set of skills than the ones he had honed in battle.

"We have already sent emissaries to the surrounding chieftains," Halfdan continued. "They will come to us soon. We need to be ready to offer them terms that will secure their loyalty while ensuring their people are content with their new rulers."

As the morning progressed, the emissaries began to arrive, each one representing a different faction from the surrounding territories. They were wary, their faces reflecting a mixture of fear and curiosity as they approached the camp. Harald observed them from a distance, noting their attire and the way they carried themselves. These were leaders used to power and respect, and they would not be easily swayed.

The first of the emissaries, a tall man with a grizzled beard named Eirik, stepped forward. His presence was imposing, and his eyes held a sharp intelligence that Harald recognized immediately. Eirik had heard of the Viking's victory and came to negotiate the terms of their future relationship.

Halfdan greeted him with the courtesy of a host and led him to a tent where negotiations would take place. Harald followed, though he remained on the outskirts of the meeting. He watched as his father and Eirik began to discuss terms, their voices low but intense. The discussion was not just about territory but also about maintaining peace and ensuring mutual benefit.

Harald noticed Eirik's skepticism, the man's eyes darting between Halfdan and Harald. It was clear that the emissary was weighing the potential benefits against the risks of aligning with the new rulers. The negotiation would be complex, and

Harald understood that it was crucial to present a compelling case for why the alliance would benefit both sides.

When the meeting concluded, Halfdan and Harald emerged, both looking satisfied but weary. Eirik had agreed to the terms, though the alliance was tentative and would require further assurances. Harald felt a sense of relief mixed with lingering apprehension. The first step toward establishing their rule had been accomplished, but many more negotiations and challenges lay ahead.

That evening, as the camp settled into a temporary peace, Harald found himself once again on the edge of the village. The devastation from the battle was still apparent, and the sight of it stirred the same feelings of unease he had experienced before. The faces of the people they had conquered, the children huddling in fear—these images weighed heavily on him.

In the quiet of the night, he found himself contemplating the future. The conquest of new lands, the expansion of their influence—it was all part of the grand plan. But Harald knew that true leadership required more than just military might. It required understanding, empathy, and the ability to unite people with a vision that went beyond mere power.

As Harald stood on the ridge overlooking the village, he thought of the future he wanted to shape. He knew that to be remembered not just as a conqueror but as a leader who brought lasting change, he would need to balance the blade with the olive branch. The new alliance was a step in the right direction, but it was only the beginning.

When he returned to the camp, Harald felt a renewed sense of purpose. He had seen the cost of victory and understood the importance of forging alliances. As the stars twinkled overhead and the firelight flickered, Harald made a silent vow to himself and to the future he hoped to build. He would strive to be a leader who not only commanded respect but also inspired trust and unity.

The road ahead would be fraught with challenges, but Harald was determined to navigate it with wisdom and strength. He had seen what conquest could do, but now he was ready to see what could be achieved through understanding and leadership. The future of his kingdom depended on it, and he was prepared to face whatever came next with the resolve to build a legacy that extended beyond the battlefield.

Chapter 9
Tides of Change

As autumn turned to winter, the world outside the camp grew colder and more unforgiving. The once verdant fjords and woodlands were now blanketed in snow, the landscape transformed into a frozen expanse of white. The change in season brought with it a period of reflection and strategic planning for Harald and his father. The victory they had won was significant, but the real work of governance and consolidation lay ahead.

The initial euphoria of conquest had faded, replaced by the steady grind of establishing control and integrating the newly acquired lands. Halfdan had retreated to his war council, poring over maps and documents, planning their next moves. Harald, now more involved in the political and administrative side of leadership, found himself immersed in the intricacies of ruling a kingdom.

The winter months were spent fortifying their new territories, building alliances, and ensuring that the local leaders remained loyal. Harald had taken to these tasks with a newfound seriousness, understanding that his actions would shape the future of their rule. The once thrilling prospect of conquest had given way to the challenges of governance—a different kind of battle, one fought with words and diplomacy rather than swords and shields.

One of the key elements in securing their rule was to address the concerns and grievances of the local population. Harald, eager to prove himself as a leader who understood the needs of his people, began holding regular meetings with the local chieftains and leaders. These meetings were not just about enforcing control but also about listening to their concerns and finding ways to address them.

During one of these meetings, Harald found himself in the presence of a particularly influential chieftain named Olav. Olav was a robust man with a deep voice and a commanding presence, known for his wisdom and experience. His lands were crucial to Harald's plans, and securing his loyalty was essential.

As Harald entered the longhouse where the meeting was to be held, he noticed Olav seated at the head of the table, flanked by his advisors. The atmosphere was formal, but there was an undercurrent of tension. Harald took a deep breath, mentally preparing himself for the discussion ahead.

"Chieftain Olav," Harald greeted, offering a respectful nod. "Thank you for agreeing to meet with me. I understand the concerns you and your people might have about the changes that are taking place."

Olav regarded Harald with a steady gaze, his eyes betraying little of his thoughts. "The changes are significant, Harald. Your father's victory has brought new rulers and new laws. My people are uneasy about what the future holds."

Harald took a seat across from Olav, his posture open and attentive. "I understand. My father's victory has altered the balance of power, and I want to assure you that our aim is to govern wisely and fairly. We want to build a kingdom that respects the traditions and needs of its people."

Olav's expression softened slightly, but he remained guarded. "Words are easy, Harald. What we need are assurances. We need to know that our lands, our people, and our traditions will be respected."

Harald nodded, recognizing the importance of Olav's concerns. "I propose a council where representatives from your people can meet with ours. We will address grievances, discuss policies, and ensure that your voice is heard in the decisions that affect your lands."

Olav considered Harald's proposal for a moment before nodding slowly. "That is a reasonable start. But we will need more than just promises. We will need to see action and commitment."

Harald felt a surge of relief. Securing Olav's agreement was a significant step toward stabilizing their rule. "You have my word, Chieftain Olav. We will work together to build a strong and equitable governance."

As the meeting concluded, Harald left the longhouse with a sense of accomplishment. The negotiations had been challenging, but they had set the stage for a more stable and cooperative relationship with the local leaders. It was a sign that their efforts to integrate and unify the newly conquered lands were beginning to bear fruit.

Back at the camp, Harald found himself reflecting on the lessons he had learned over the past months. The transition from a warrior to a ruler had been demanding, but it had also been enlightening. He had come to understand that true leadership involved more than just winning battles—it required the ability to listen, negotiate, and build lasting relationships.

One evening, as Harald walked along the frozen shoreline, the icy wind stinging his face, he saw a familiar figure approaching. It was Sigurd, the warrior who had spoken to him during the early days of their conquest.

"Harald," Sigurd called out, falling into step beside him. "You've done well. The alliances are forming, and the local leaders are beginning to see the benefits of our rule."

Harald smiled, though his thoughts were still troubled. "Thank you, Sigurd. But there's much work still to be done. The real challenge is in maintaining these alliances and ensuring that we continue to lead with integrity."

Sigurd nodded in agreement. "Indeed. And it's not just about what you do as a leader, but how you are remembered. The legacy you build will be what people talk about long after we're gone."

The words struck a chord with Harald. He had always been focused on the immediate challenges, the battles to be won and the territories to be secured. But now, he began to see the broader picture—the impact of his actions on the future of his kingdom and his place in history.

As the days grew shorter and the nights colder, Harald continued to navigate the complexities of leadership. He spent time with local leaders, addressed grievances, and worked to solidify the new alliances. His efforts were beginning to show results, and the stability they had sought was slowly taking shape.

The winter was a time of reflection and preparation. Harald knew that the coming spring would bring new opportunities and challenges. As he looked out over the frozen fjords, he felt a sense of determination. He was forging a path that would shape the future of his kingdom, and he was committed to making that path one of strength, unity, and respect.

Chapter 10
Winter's Peace

As winter tightened its grip on the land, Harald Fairhair found himself navigating a delicate balance between consolidating power and maintaining the fragile peace that had been established. The snow-covered landscapes were serene but belied the complex political maneuvers that were ongoing. With the chill came a period of reflection and strategy, a time when Harald could assess the progress of his rule and prepare for the challenges that lay ahead.

In the heart of the camp, Harald's quarters had become a hub of activity. The tent was now filled with maps, documents, and a collection of gifts and treaties from the neighboring chieftains. The camp itself, though smaller in winter, was a hive of quiet industry, with men working on fortifications, gathering supplies, and preparing for the next phase of their expansion.

One morning, as Harald reviewed a stack of reports, his father entered the tent, his presence immediately commanding attention. Halfdan's face was weathered but his eyes sparkled with the same fierce energy that had driven him through countless battles. Despite the cold, there was a warmth in the way he approached his son, a sign of the pride he felt in Harald's achievements.

"How are the negotiations going?" Halfdan asked, settling into a chair and looking over the documents spread out before Harald.

Harald looked up, his brow furrowed in concentration. "We've secured several alliances and managed to address most of the grievances from the local leaders. There are still a few holdouts, but I believe we can bring them into the fold with continued efforts."

Halfdan nodded, his expression thoughtful. "You've done well. This winter is crucial for laying the groundwork for what comes next. We need to ensure that our alliances are strong and that the people see the benefits of our rule."

Harald agreed, knowing that the real work was only beginning. The winter months were an opportunity to solidify their position and prepare for the spring, when the harshness of winter would give way to the renewed vigor of the land. It was also a time to address the internal issues that had arisen during their conquests and to ensure that the new governance structures were effective.

One of the pressing concerns was the integration of the local populations into their rule. The winter had brought with it a lull in military activity, which allowed Harald to focus on these issues more closely. He had organized councils with local leaders to discuss the administration of justice, the allocation of resources, and the preservation of cultural practices.

During one such council, Harald met with a group of local elders from a village that had been deeply affected by the recent conflicts. The elders were wary but hopeful, their faces etched with the lines of age and experience. They had come to discuss their grievances and to seek assurances about their future under Harald's rule.

Harald welcomed them into his tent, offering them warm drinks and a place by the fire. The atmosphere was more relaxed than it had been during their earlier meetings. Harald had learned that gaining the trust of these leaders required more than just promises—it required showing them respect and a genuine willingness to address their concerns.

"Thank you for coming," Harald began, his tone earnest. "I want to hear from you directly about the issues you and your people are facing. It's important to me that we work together to find solutions."

The eldest of the group, a woman with a dignified air and a sharp gaze, spoke up. "We have seen many changes in our lives since your father's victory. Some of these changes have been beneficial, but others have caused hardship. We need to ensure that our traditions are respected and that our people are treated fairly."

Harald listened attentively, nodding as the elders spoke. He understood the importance of maintaining the balance between progress and tradition. The integration of new territories into their realm had to be done carefully, with an eye toward preserving what was valuable while introducing new systems of governance.

"We will work to ensure that your traditions are respected," Harald promised. "We will also provide support where it is needed to help you adjust to the new administration. I believe that by working together, we can create a stable and prosperous future for everyone."

The elders seemed reassured by Harald's commitment. They discussed various issues, ranging from land disputes to the distribution of resources. The conversation was productive, and by the end of the meeting, there was a renewed sense of hope among the leaders.

As the winter progressed, Harald continued to focus on building these relationships and addressing the needs of the people. He visited various villages, spoke with local leaders, and worked on strengthening the alliances that had been formed. The effort was demanding, but it was necessary to ensure that the kingdom would be stable and unified when the spring arrived.

One evening, as Harald walked through the camp, he noticed the quiet beauty of the snow-covered landscape. The camp was bustling with activity, but there was a sense of peace in the stillness of the night. The world seemed to be holding its breath, waiting for the next chapter of their journey.

Harald took a moment to reflect on the progress they had made. The battles had been won, the alliances secured, and the governance structures put in place. The challenges ahead were significant, but Harald felt a sense of optimism. The work done during the winter would lay the foundation for a stronger and more unified kingdom.

As he gazed out over the snow-covered landscape, Harald made a silent vow to continue working for the future of his people. The path he had chosen was fraught with difficulties, but he was determined to navigate it with wisdom and resolve. The legacy he hoped to build was not just one of conquest but of lasting peace and prosperity.

The winter's peace was a time of preparation and reflection. It was a time to lay the groundwork for the future, to build relationships, and to ensure that the kingdom would be ready for the challenges and opportunities that the spring would bring.

Chapter 11
Awakening Spring

As winter's grip slowly loosened and the first signs of spring began to emerge, Harald Fairhair felt a renewed sense of anticipation and energy. The thawing ice and the melting snow heralded the beginning of a new chapter for the kingdom. The once-frozen fjords were now starting to break up, revealing the dark waters beneath. The snow-covered land was gradually being replaced by patches of green, and the air was filled with the promise of renewal and growth.

The transition from winter to spring was not just a change in weather but a critical period for Harald and his father. It was a time to capitalize on the alliances that had been formed, to consolidate power, and to prepare for any potential challenges that might arise as the world awakened from its long slumber. The thaw brought with it both opportunities and uncertainties, and Harald knew that how they managed this transition would shape the future of their kingdom.

One morning, as the first rays of sunlight pierced through the remaining frost, Harald gathered his advisors and local leaders for a meeting. The mood was one of cautious optimism. The spring thaw had freed the waterways, making it possible to resume trade and communication with other regions. The prospect of renewed activity and growth was invigorating, but it also brought with it the need for careful planning.

Halfdan, looking more vibrant with the change in season, addressed the gathering with a sense of urgency and excitement. "The arrival of spring marks a new beginning for us. The land is waking up, and so must we. It is time to put our plans into action and to ensure that our alliances are solid and our governance effective."

Harald nodded in agreement, his thoughts focused on the tasks ahead. "With the thaw, we have the opportunity to reestablish trade routes, strengthen our alliances, and address any remaining issues from the winter. It's crucial that we use this time wisely."

The meeting turned to discussions about the various projects and initiatives that needed to be undertaken. One of the primary focuses was the rebuilding of infrastructure that had been damaged or neglected during the winter. The thaw had revealed the full extent of the damage, and it was clear that significant work was needed to repair roads, fortify defenses, and restore vital services.

Another critical area of focus was the integration of the newly acquired territories. The local leaders had expressed their concerns during the winter, and Harald was determined to address them effectively. The goal was to ensure that the people felt secure and valued under the new rule, and that the transition was smooth and beneficial for everyone involved.

As the days grew longer and warmer, Harald found himself increasingly engaged in the practical aspects of leadership. He visited various parts of the kingdom, observing the progress of the rebuilding efforts and meeting with local leaders to discuss their concerns. The spring thaw had brought with it a flurry of activity, and Harald was at the center of it all, working tirelessly to ensure that the kingdom's transition was successful.

One afternoon, Harald rode out to a village that had been heavily affected by the winter's hardships. The villagers had been struggling with shortages of supplies and difficulties in transportation. Harald's visit was intended to offer support and to reassure them that their needs would be addressed.

The village was bustling with activity as Harald arrived, the people working to repair homes and clear the debris left by the winter. The sight of

Harald and his entourage was met with a mixture of relief and curiosity. Harald dismounted and approached the village elder, a woman named Ingrid who had been a vocal advocate for her people's needs.

"Elder Ingrid," Harald greeted her warmly. "I have come to see how you and your people are faring and to offer any assistance we can provide."

Ingrid welcomed Harald with a nod of appreciation. "We are grateful for your visit, Harald. The winter has been harsh, but with the spring, we are beginning to recover. There are still challenges, but your presence here brings us hope."

Harald spent the day with Ingrid and the other villagers, listening to their concerns and discussing potential solutions. The discussions were productive, and Harald was able to offer immediate assistance in the form of supplies and resources. He also made promises to address longer-term issues, such as improving infrastructure and ensuring that their needs were met.

As he prepared to leave the village, Harald felt a sense of accomplishment. The visit had strengthened his connection with the people and reaffirmed his commitment to their well-being. The challenges of the winter were beginning to fade, and the promise of a new beginning was taking shape.

Returning to the camp, Harald found that the work of rebuilding and preparing for the future was well underway. The thaw had invigorated everyone, and there was a renewed sense of purpose and energy. The spring was not just a change in the seasons but a symbol of the fresh start that lay ahead.

Harald knew that the coming months would be crucial in solidifying their rule and ensuring that the kingdom was ready for the challenges of the future. The thaw had brought with it new opportunities, but it also required careful management and strategic planning.

As he looked out over the landscape, Harald felt a renewed sense of determination. The path ahead was filled with possibilities, and he was ready to face them with the same courage and resolve that had carried him through the battles and negotiations of the past.

Chapter 12
The Battle Cry

The arrival of summer brought with it not only the full bloom of the land but also the simmering tensions of the region. Harald Fairhair, now firmly established as a leader, faced the realities of maintaining his kingdom's integrity amidst ongoing rivalries and dissent. The thawing of the ice had reinvigorated the local chieftains and enemies who sought to challenge Harald's newfound power.

Word reached Harald that a formidable rival, Jarl Hakon, had been gathering forces in the southern fjords, planning an assault on the territories under Harald's control. The intelligence suggested that Jarl Hakon's forces were well-equipped and numerous, presenting a serious threat to the stability that Harald had worked so hard to establish.

Harald wasted no time in preparing for the conflict. He rallied his own forces, calling upon the loyal warriors who had stood by him through the trials of war and governance. The camp buzzed with activity as soldiers sharpened their weapons, repaired their armor, and readied their ships. The air was thick with a mixture of anticipation and unease, a prelude to the violence that was to come.

The day of the battle dawned with a heavy mist hanging over the fjords. Harald, clad in his armor and mounted on his warhorse, surveyed his troops as they assembled. The landscape was both beautiful and foreboding, the tranquil waters of the fjord contrasting sharply with the impending clash of arms.

As the morning sun began to burn through the mist, Harald and his army moved out, their ships cutting through the water with purpose. The plan was to confront Jarl Hakon's forces head-on, using the element of surprise to their advantage. Harald's heart pounded with a mix of adrenaline and resolve. This battle was not just a test of his military prowess but a crucial moment for securing his legacy.

The two forces met at a narrow strait, the waters churned by the activity of the approaching fleets. The sight of Jarl Hakon's ships, dark and imposing against the backdrop of the fjord, brought a steely determination to Harald's eyes. He could see the enemy preparing for the confrontation, their banners fluttering in the wind and their warriors readying for the fight.

As Harald's ships closed in, the tension reached a fever pitch. The roar of battle preparations and the clamor of armor being adjusted filled the air. Harald, standing at the prow of his flagship, could feel the gravity of the moment. He turned to his men, his voice ringing out with authority.

"Today, we fight not just for our lands but for our honor! Show them the strength of our resolve and the might of our unity!"

His words were met with a chorus of shouts and the clanging of weapons, a palpable surge of energy among his troops. The battle began with the clash of steel against steel, the air filled with the cacophony of war. Harald's warriors fought valiantly, their movements coordinated and fierce.

In the heat of the battle, Harald's focus was unyielding. He moved through the fray with a determined purpose, his sword flashing as he cut through the enemy lines. The chaos of the battlefield seemed almost secondary to his singular goal: to face Jarl Hakon and end the threat decisively.

It was during a particularly fierce engagement that Harald finally came face-to-face with Jarl Hakon. The rival jarl, a burly figure with a fierce countenance, was engaged in a brutal duel with one of Harald's champions. Harald watched, his gaze fixed on the man who had caused so much unrest.

Seizing the opportunity, Harald charged forward, pushing through the throng of combatants until he stood directly before Jarl Hakon. The two men locked eyes, the intensity of their rivalry palpable. Without hesitation, Harald let out a guttural scream, a primal roar that echoed across the battlefield. It was a cry of pure rage and defiance, a sound that seemed to shake the very air.

The scream was more than a battle cry—it was a declaration of his resolve and a challenge to his enemy. Jarl Hakon, momentarily taken aback by the ferocity of Harald's cry, raised his weapon in response. The clash between the two leaders was immediate and intense. Harald's sword met Hakon's with a resounding clang, sparks flying as the blades collided.

The duel was fierce and unrelenting. Harald fought with a blend of practiced skill and raw emotion, driven by the need to protect his realm and to assert his authority. His movements were precise and powerful, each strike and parry executed with the weight of his resolve. Jarl Hakon was a formidable opponent, but Harald's determination and strength began to turn the tide.

In a final, decisive moment, Harald delivered a powerful blow that sent Hakon sprawling to the ground. The enemy jarl struggled to rise, but Harald was upon him, his sword poised for the finishing strike. With a deep breath and a grim expression, Harald brought his sword down, ending the confrontation.

The roar of victory that followed was deafening. Harald's troops, witnessing their leader's triumph, surged forward with renewed vigor. The tide of the battle had turned, and the enemy forces, disheartened by the loss of their leader, began to retreat.

As the battle came to a close, Harald stood amidst the aftermath, his armor stained and his breath heavy. The victory was hard-won, and the cost had been significant. But the sight of his victorious men and the knowledge that his kingdom was secure brought a deep sense of satisfaction.

The victory over Jarl Hakon was more than just a military success; it was a crucial moment in Harald's journey as a leader. It reaffirmed his strength, his resolve, and his ability to defend his realm against those who sought to undermine it. As he looked out over the battlefield, Harald knew that this victory would be remembered as a defining moment in his rise to power.

Chapter 13
Union of Strength

The aftermath of the battle was marked by both celebration and reflection. Harald Fairhair's victory over Jarl Hakon solidified his position and brought a measure of peace to the realm. The summer had proven to be a season of triumph and consolidation, but it was also a time for Harald to turn his attention to matters of personal and political importance.

As the days grew longer and the fields began to ripen, Harald realized that a strategic alliance through marriage could strengthen his rule even further. Though he had established his dominance through force, securing a marriage alliance would help solidify his control and bring greater stability to the kingdom.

Harald's choice of bride was driven by both political strategy and personal considerations. Among the prominent families of the region, the daughter of King Eirik of the neighboring kingdom of Jutland stood out. Her name was Astrid, known for her beauty, intelligence, and noble lineage. The union with Astrid would not only create a powerful alliance but also demonstrate Harald's commitment to peace and stability.

Negotiations for the marriage were conducted with great care. Harald sent emissaries to Jutland to propose the match, emphasizing the benefits of the alliance for both kingdoms. The discussions were thorough, with attention paid to the terms of the marriage, the dowry, and the political implications. The agreement was reached, and the engagement was announced with great ceremony.

The preparations for the wedding were elaborate. The festivities were planned to be grand, reflecting the significance of the union. Harald's advisors worked tirelessly to ensure that every detail was perfect, from the decorations to the feasts. The wedding was to be held in a specially constructed hall that showcased the splendor of Harald's realm, a testament to his growing power and influence.

On the day of the wedding, the air was filled with excitement and anticipation. The hall was adorned with rich tapestries and flowers, the colors and scents creating a vibrant and celebratory atmosphere. Guests from across the region arrived, dressed in their finest attire, their presence a testament to the importance of the event.

Harald, dressed in ceremonial armor and a richly embroidered cloak, stood at the entrance of the hall, his gaze scanning the crowd. His heart swelled with a mixture of pride and anticipation. He had seen Astrid only a few times before, but he knew that their union was a crucial step in securing the future of his kingdom.

As Astrid entered the hall, she was greeted with admiration and respect. Her beauty was undeniable, and her poise commanded attention. She wore a gown of deep blue, accentuated by intricate silver embroidery that reflected her royal status. The guests watched in awe as she walked down the aisle, her presence adding a sense of grace and dignity to the proceedings.

The ceremony itself was a blend of solemnity and joy. The vows were exchanged with sincerity, and the words spoken were filled with promises of loyalty and partnership. Harald and Astrid stood before the assembled guests, their hands joined as they declared their commitment to one another. The officiant's words resonated through the hall, marking the union of two powerful houses and the beginning of a new chapter in their lives.

As the ceremony concluded, the newlyweds were escorted to the head of the grand hall, where the feast awaited. The celebration was a grand affair, with music, dancing, and an array of sumptuous dishes. The guests enjoyed the festivities, their laughter and conversation filling the hall. The atmosphere was one of unity and optimism, reflecting the hopes for a prosperous future.

During the feast, Harald and Astrid took time to mingle with their guests, sharing stories and forging connections. The union of their houses was seen as a symbol of strength and cooperation, and the celebrations were a reflection of the positive future that both parties anticipated.

As the evening progressed, Harald and Astrid shared a quiet moment away from the revelry. They walked through the gardens, where the first blossoms of summer were beginning to bloom. The tranquility of the garden offered a contrast to the exuberance of the hall, and the couple enjoyed a brief respite from the festivities.

Harald turned to Astrid, his expression softening. "Today has been a significant step for both of us. I am grateful for your presence and the strength you bring to our alliance."

Astrid smiled, her eyes reflecting both warmth and resolve. "I share your sentiments, Harald. This union holds great promise, and I am committed to supporting you in all that lies ahead."

The bond between Harald and Astrid was more than just a political alliance; it was a partnership built on mutual respect and shared goals. As they walked through the garden, the future seemed bright and full of potential.

The wedding marked a new beginning for Harald Fairhair. It was not only a personal milestone but also a strategic move that would enhance his rule and bring greater stability to his kingdom. The union with Astrid was a testament to his ability to navigate both the political and personal aspects of leadership.

As the summer days grew warmer and the fields flourished, Harald looked forward to the future with a renewed sense of purpose. The challenges of the past had been met with determination, and the promise of new opportunities lay ahead. With Astrid by his side, Harald was ready to face whatever came next, confident in the strength of their union and the bright future they would build together.

Chapter 14
Shadows of
Dissent

With the marriage of Harald Fairhair and Astrid of Jutland, the kingdom entered a period of relative stability and prosperity. The union had bolstered Harald's position, forging stronger ties with Jutland and securing a more unified front against potential adversaries. The summer was filled with joyous festivities and strategic planning, setting the stage for a promising future.

Yet, beneath the surface of this apparent tranquility, there were undercurrents of dissent and unease. The consolidation of Harald's power had not been universally accepted, and there were still factions within the realm who resented his dominance. Some of the rival chieftains and nobles, feeling their influence wane in the face of Harald's growing strength, began to stir discontent among their followers.

One such figure was Eirik, a once-powerful chieftain who had lost much of his land and influence during Harald's rise. Eirik, nursing a deep grudge against the new regime, began to quietly rally his supporters. He sought to exploit the dissatisfaction that simmered among those who felt sidelined by Harald's unification efforts. The whispers of rebellion grew louder, and it became clear that not everyone was content with the new order.

Harald was not oblivious to these signs of unrest. He had always been keenly aware of the delicate balance between maintaining control and addressing the grievances of his subjects. The challenge now was to address the brewing discontent before it erupted into open conflict. He convened a council of trusted advisors and allies to discuss the situation and devise a strategy to deal with the potential threat.

The council meeting was held in the grand hall of Harald's stronghold. The room was filled with an air of tension as the advisors gathered to hear the latest reports. Harald, seated at the head of the table, listened intently as his chief advisor, Thrain, presented the intelligence.

"Eirik's movements are becoming more noticeable," Thrain reported. "He has been meeting with discontented chieftains and stirring unrest among the local population. His goal appears to be to undermine your authority and create instability."

Harald frowned, his mind working through the implications of this new threat. "What is our assessment of his support? How widespread is the discontent?"

Another advisor, Brynhild, spoke up. "The discontent is not universal, but it is significant enough to be a concern. Eirik has managed to tap into the grievances of those who feel marginalized by the new order. His support is growing, and we cannot afford to ignore it."

Harald nodded, understanding the gravity of the situation. "We need to address this issue decisively. If left unchecked, it could undermine the stability we have worked so hard to achieve. What are our options?"

The advisors discussed various strategies, ranging from diplomatic outreach to military intervention. Harald knew that a nuanced approach was necessary. A heavy-handed response might inflame the situation further, while a purely diplomatic approach might not be sufficient to quell the rebellion. The key was to find a balance that would restore order without alienating the broader population.

After much deliberation, Harald decided to take a dual approach. He would engage in diplomatic efforts to address the grievances of those who felt wronged, while simultaneously preparing for the possibility of military action if the situation escalated. He dispatched envoys to Eirik and his supporters, seeking to negotiate and address their concerns. At the same time, he began to reinforce his own defenses and ensure that his loyal forces were prepared for any potential conflict.

The diplomatic efforts were met with a mixture of skepticism and cautious optimism. Eirik and his supporters were willing to engage in negotiations, but they were also wary of Harald's intentions. The discussions were tense, with both sides expressing their grievances and demands. Harald approached the negotiations with a genuine desire to understand and address the underlying issues, but he also made it clear that any attempt to undermine his authority would be met with a firm response.

As the negotiations continued, the situation remained volatile. Eirik's rhetoric and actions kept the region on edge, and the potential for open conflict was ever-present. Harald and his advisors worked tirelessly to manage the crisis, balancing the need for diplomacy with the necessity of preparedness.

In the midst of this turmoil, Harald found solace in the support of his wife, Astrid. Her presence was a source of strength and encouragement, and her counsel proved invaluable. Astrid had a keen understanding of the political landscape and offered insights that helped Harald navigate the complex situation.

One evening, as Harald and Astrid walked through the gardens of their stronghold, the weight of the situation was evident in Harald's demeanor. He confided in Astrid about his concerns and the challenges he faced.

"I worry that we may be heading towards a larger conflict," Harald admitted. "Eirik's actions and the growing discontent are unsettling. I fear that our efforts to stabilize the kingdom may be unraveling."

Astrid placed a reassuring hand on his arm. "You have always faced challenges with courage and wisdom, Harald. The situation is difficult, but you have the support of your people and the strength to see it through. We must remain steadfast and continue to address both the grievances and the threats."

Harald nodded, drawing strength from her words. "Thank you, Astrid. Your support means more than you know."

The coming weeks would test Harald's resolve and leadership. The threat of rebellion loomed large, and the need to navigate the complexities of diplomacy and military strategy was paramount. As he prepared for the challenges ahead, Harald remained committed to securing the future of his kingdom and ensuring that the stability he had worked so hard to achieve was not undone.

The chapter ahead would be one of intense struggle and decisive action. Harald Fairhair was prepared to confront the shadows of dissent and to uphold the unity and strength of his realm, guided by the principles of leadership and the support of those closest to him.

Chapter 15
Gathering Storm

As autumn settled over the kingdom, the air grew crisp and the leaves turned shades of gold and crimson. The season of harvest brought with it both a bounty of crops and a deepening of the unrest that had begun to brew in the summer. The negotiations with Eirik had yielded little progress, and the simmering discontent had evolved into a more organized challenge to Harald Fairhair's rule.

The increasing dissatisfaction among some of the chieftains and nobles had reached a critical point. Eirik, having built a coalition of discontented leaders, was now openly challenging Harald's authority. The discontented factions had begun to act with greater boldness, conducting raids on Harald's loyal territories and spreading propaganda that sought to undermine his legitimacy.

Harald knew that the time for mere diplomacy had passed. He called for an assembly of his most trusted commanders and advisors to discuss the next steps. The gathering was held in a fortified hall, designed to withstand the threat of attack. The atmosphere was charged with urgency as Harald outlined the situation and sought counsel on how to address the growing threat.

"The unrest is spreading," Harald said, his voice steady but carrying an edge of concern. "Eirik and his allies are actively challenging our control. Their raids are becoming more frequent and more coordinated. We cannot afford to let this situation escalate further."

His chief advisor, Thrain, spoke first. "We need to act decisively. Eirik's rebellion has gained momentum, and the longer we wait, the more difficult it will be to quell. A show of strength may be necessary to restore order."

Brynhild, another trusted advisor, nodded in agreement. "We should consider a two-pronged approach. First, we reinforce our defenses and prepare for a potential military confrontation. Second, we continue to reach out to those who might still be swayed to our side. There are always factions that remain neutral or undecided."

The discussion was intense, with differing opinions on the best course of action. Some advisors favored a direct military response, arguing that a decisive battle would crush the rebellion and restore Harald's authority. Others suggested a more measured approach, focusing on diplomacy and attempting to negotiate with Eirik's supporters.

After a thorough debate, Harald made his decision. He would prepare for a military campaign to confront Eirik and his allies, while also continuing diplomatic efforts to isolate the rebellious factions and win over any undecided chieftains. It was a strategy that balanced strength with diplomacy, aimed at addressing the immediate threat while also working to secure long-term stability.

The preparations for the military campaign began in earnest. Harald's forces were mobilized, and the stronghold was fortified to withstand any potential siege. The soldiers drilled tirelessly, their training reflecting the seriousness of the impending conflict. Harald personally oversaw the preparations, ensuring that his troops were well-equipped and ready for the challenges ahead.

Simultaneously, Harald sent emissaries to the remaining neutral factions, attempting to persuade them to support his cause. The negotiations were complex and often fraught with difficulty, but Harald's reputation and the tangible benefits of loyalty to his regime provided a compelling argument.

As the campaign neared its launch, Harald received word of a significant development. Eirik had begun to consolidate his forces, and a large-scale confrontation seemed imminent. The two sides were preparing for a decisive clash, with both sides eager to demonstrate their strength and resolve.

The night before the battle, Harald stood alone on a high vantage point overlooking his camp. The sky was a deep indigo, dotted with stars that seemed distant and indifferent. The camp was quiet, the usual bustle of activity subdued as the troops prepared for the confrontation. Harald's thoughts were heavy with the weight of leadership and the responsibility of protecting his realm.

Astrid joined him, her presence a calming influence amidst the tension. She placed a hand on his shoulder, her touch grounding him. "You have prepared well, Harald. The coming battle will test our resolve, but I have faith in your leadership."

Harald turned to her, his expression one of both gratitude and resolve. "Thank you, Astrid. Your support means everything to me. We face a challenging path ahead, but we will face it together."

The dawn of the following day broke with a sense of finality. The armies assembled, each side preparing for the clash that would determine the future of the kingdom. Harald's troops, steadfast and ready, formed ranks as the banners of the opposing forces became visible on the horizon.

The battlefield, a vast open area surrounded by rolling hills and rocky outcrops, was soon filled with the sounds of preparation—the clatter of armor, the murmur of orders, and the distant calls of commanders rallying their troops. The tension was palpable, each side readying for the confrontation that would decide their fate.

As the armies faced off, the air was charged with anticipation. The conflict that had been simmering for months was about to erupt into full-scale combat. Harald knew that this battle would be a defining moment, one that would either solidify his authority or challenge his vision of a unified kingdom.

The battle began with a thunderous clash as the two sides collided. The initial engagements were fierce, with both armies demonstrating their determination and skill. Harald fought with the intensity and precision that had come to define his leadership. His presence on the battlefield was both inspiring and formidable, his every move calculated to lead his forces to victory.

As the battle raged on, Harald's strategy began to unfold. His forces pressed the attack, exploiting weaknesses in the enemy's lines and applying relentless pressure. The confrontation was brutal, with heavy losses on both sides, but Harald's determination and tactical acumen began to turn the tide.

In the midst of the chaos, Harald faced Eirik once more. The two leaders clashed in a dramatic confrontation, their battle cries echoing across the field. The struggle was intense, each man fighting with the weight of their ambitions and the fate of their people hanging in the balance.

With a final, decisive strike, Harald overcame Eirik, ending the immediate threat of rebellion. The victory was hard-won, and the battlefield was strewn with the remnants of the fierce conflict. Harald's forces emerged triumphant, but the cost of the battle was significant, and the work of rebuilding and consolidating would begin anew.

As the dust settled, Harald looked out over the battlefield, reflecting on the trials he had faced and the path that lay ahead. The victory was a crucial step in securing his realm, but the challenges of leadership and the need for unity remained. With Astrid by his side and the support of his loyal followers, Harald prepared to face the future with renewed determination.

The storm had passed, but the journey was far from over. Harald Fairhair had weathered the gathering storm and emerged victorious, but the task of forging a lasting peace and ensuring the stability of his kingdom would require continued effort and resolve. The path forward was one of both opportunity and challenge, and Harald was ready to navigate it with the strength and wisdom that had defined his leadership.

Chapter 16
Dawn of unity

The decisive battle against Eirik and his rebellious coalition had left a mark on both the land and Harald Fairhair. The aftermath of the conflict was a period of intense reflection and reorganization. The victory had restored Harald's control but had come at a steep cost, both in terms of lives lost and the strain on his resources.

The realm was weary from the prolonged conflict, and Harald knew that securing lasting peace required more than just military triumph. The path to unity would involve healing the divisions that had been exacerbated by the rebellion and rebuilding trust among the various factions of his kingdom.

In the weeks following the battle, Harald set about the monumental task of reconciliation and reconstruction. His first step was to address the concerns of the local leaders and chieftains who had supported Eirik. Harald understood that simply defeating the rebellion was not enough; he needed to demonstrate that his rule would be fair and inclusive, offering opportunities for those who were willing to align with the new order.

Harald summoned a council of the most influential leaders from across the kingdom, including those who had been involved in the rebellion. The gathering was held in the great hall of his stronghold, which had been meticulously prepared to accommodate the diverse group of attendees. The atmosphere was charged with a mixture of apprehension and hope as the leaders took their seats.

Harald began the council with a speech that emphasized his commitment to a unified realm. "The recent conflict has shown us the strength of our resolve but also the deep divisions that exist among us. We must now turn our focus to healing those rifts and building a kingdom that works for all its people. Our future depends on our ability to come together and work as one."

His words were met with a mixture of nods and murmurs, and Harald could see that the assembly was receptive but cautious. He continued, outlining his vision for a more inclusive governance structure that would provide a voice for all factions, including those who had opposed him.

In addition to political reforms, Harald proposed a series of practical measures to address the immediate needs of the realm. These included rebuilding infrastructure damaged during the conflict, restoring trade routes that had been disrupted, and providing aid to the families affected by the war. By addressing these practical concerns, Harald aimed to demonstrate his commitment to the welfare of his subjects and to ease the process of reconciliation.

The council was a success, and many of the leaders who had once opposed Harald began to show willingness to cooperate. The process of rebuilding trust was gradual, but Harald's approach of fairness and inclusivity helped to pave the way for a more unified kingdom. The changes implemented during this period helped to stabilize the realm and set the stage for a new era of relative peace and prosperity.

Amidst the political and social restructuring, Harald found time to reflect on the personal aspects of his life. The victory and the subsequent responsibilities had kept him occupied, but he made a point to spend quality time with his wife, Astrid. Their relationship had been a source of strength throughout the challenges they had faced, and Harald valued the moments of solace they found together.

One evening, as the autumn leaves fell around them, Harald and Astrid walked through the gardens of their stronghold. The quiet of the garden was a welcome contrast to the bustle of their daily duties. They spoke of their hopes for the future and the role they envisioned for their children in the realm they were working to build.

"We have come through much together," Astrid said, her voice soft. "And now we have the opportunity to shape the future of our kingdom. What kind of legacy do you hope we will leave behind?"

Harald pondered her question, his gaze fixed on the horizon. "I hope that our legacy will be one of unity and strength. That we will be remembered not just for the battles we fought but for the peace we forged. Our children will inherit this realm, and I want them to grow up in a land that is prosperous and united."

Astrid nodded, her eyes reflecting her own hopes. "I believe we are on the right path. The challenges we have faced have strengthened us, and together we can create a future that honors the sacrifices made and the dreams we hold."

As the days turned into months, the realm began to recover from the turmoil of the past. The economy improved, trade resumed, and the people slowly regained their sense of stability. Harald's efforts to create a more inclusive and equitable governance structure helped to foster a sense of shared purpose and commitment among his subjects.

The kingdom entered a period of renewal, with the focus shifting from conflict to development. Harald and Astrid continued to work together to ensure that the advancements made during this time were built upon and sustained. Their leadership was characterized by a dedication to the well-being of their people and a vision for a unified and prosperous realm.

In the years that followed, Harald's legacy as a unifier and a leader began to take shape. The stability and prosperity achieved during his reign set the foundation for future generations. The kingdom flourished under his guidance, and the values of unity and fairness he championed became deeply ingrained in the fabric of the realm.

As Harald looked back on his journey, he saw a land transformed by his efforts and the support of those around him. The challenges faced had been formidable, but they had also been the crucible in which his leadership and vision were tested. The dawn of unity had arrived, and Harald Fairhair had played a pivotal role in shaping the course of history for his people.

Chapter 17
Passing the Torch

As Harald Fairhair approached the twilight years of his reign, the kingdom was enjoying a period of relative peace and prosperity. His efforts to unite and stabilize the realm had paid off, creating a foundation for a future that promised continued stability and growth. With the kingdom firmly in his control, Harald began to contemplate his legacy and the transition of power to the next generation.

Harald's children had grown into capable and promising individuals, each demonstrating qualities that reflected their father's strengths and values. His eldest son, Erik, had become a respected leader in his own right, known for his strategic acumen and commitment to the kingdom's welfare. His other children, including Haakon and Ragnhild, were also making their marks, each contributing to the realm in their own ways.

The decision to retire was not one Harald made lightly. He had dedicated his life to the service of his people, and the thought of stepping down from the throne was accompanied by a sense of both relief and apprehension. He wanted to ensure that his successor would be ready to take on the responsibilities of leadership and continue the work he had started.

Harald convened a family meeting to discuss his plans for retirement and the transition of power. The gathering was held in the grand hall of his stronghold, a place filled with memories of past victories and decisions. The atmosphere was a mixture of anticipation and solemnity as Harald addressed his children.

"My dear children," Harald began, his voice resonant with the weight of his words. "The time has come for me to step down from the throne. I have spent my life guiding this kingdom, and now it is time for a new generation to lead. I have great confidence in each of you and believe that you are well-prepared to carry on the legacy we have built."

Erik, the eldest, stood at the forefront of the discussion. His demeanor was one of respectful attentiveness, but his eyes betrayed a flicker of concern. "Father, are you certain this is the right time? The kingdom is thriving under your leadership, and I worry about the challenges we might face in the transition."

Harald nodded, understanding Erik's concerns. "I have considered this deeply. I believe that the time is right for a new leader to guide the kingdom forward. I trust in your abilities and those of your siblings. My role now is to provide guidance and support as you prepare for this transition."

Haakon, known for his diplomatic skills, spoke next. "Father, we are ready to support Erik and each other in this transition. We have learned much from you and are prepared to continue your work. Our focus will be on maintaining the unity and prosperity you have established."

Ragnhild, the youngest, expressed her thoughts with a mix of determination and sentiment. "We are grateful for your leadership and the opportunities you have given us. We will honor your legacy by continuing to work together and uphold the values you have instilled in us."

Harald's heart swelled with pride as he listened to his children. Their responses reflected the strength and unity he had hoped for, and he felt reassured about the future of the kingdom. "Your support and commitment mean everything to me. I have no doubt that you will handle the responsibilities with wisdom and integrity."

The family discussion was followed by a series of formal preparations for Harald's retirement. The transition of power was managed with careful planning to ensure a smooth handover. Erik was officially designated as the new king, and the ceremonies marking this change were conducted with the pomp and reverence befitting such a significant event.

As Erik assumed the throne, Harald took on a more advisory role, focusing on offering counsel and support while stepping back from the day-to-day governance. He remained a respected figure in the kingdom, his wisdom and experience continuing to influence the decisions made by the new leadership.

The transition was not without its challenges. Erik and his siblings had to navigate the complexities of ruling a realm that had been shaped by their father's efforts. There were still external threats and internal issues to address, and the new leaders worked diligently to ensure that the kingdom remained strong and unified.

Despite the challenges, Harald found satisfaction in watching his children step into their roles. The kingdom continued to flourish under their stewardship, and Harald's legacy endured through their leadership. He took solace in knowing that the values and principles he had championed were being carried forward by the next generation.

In his retirement, Harald spent more time with his family, enjoying moments of reflection and camaraderie. He shared stories of his experiences and offered guidance when sought, but he also took pleasure in witnessing the growth and accomplishments of his children.

One evening, as Harald sat with Astrid in the quiet of their garden, he reflected on the journey of his life. The kingdom he had built was now in the hands of capable leaders, and the legacy he had worked so hard to create was being carried forward.

"It is a strange feeling, stepping away from the role I have held for so long," Harald said. "But I am proud of what we have achieved and confident in the future."

Astrid smiled, her hand resting gently on his. "You have given everything to this kingdom, and now it is time for you to enjoy the fruits of your labor. Your legacy will live on through your children and the realm you have shaped."

Harald nodded, content with the knowledge that his life's work had set the stage for a promising future. The chapter of his reign had come to a close, but the story of his impact on the kingdom and his family would continue to be remembered and celebrated for generations to come.

The Legend:

Demystified

Outline:

Introduction to Harald Fairhair

- Harald Fairhair, also known as Harald I of Norway, is regarded as the first king to unify Norway.
- His life merges historical facts with legend, laying the foundation for the Norwegian kingdom during the late 9th and early 10th centuries.

Early Life and Rise to Power

- Born around 850 AD as the son of Halfdan the Black, a local king in southeastern Norway.
- Inherited his father's realm after his death and embarked on a campaign to unite the fragmented petty kingdoms of Norway.

The Legend of the Hair

- Harald's vow to not cut his hair until he unified Norway led to his nickname "Fairhair" (Harald Hårfagre).

- The legend states that his pursuit of Gyda, who refused his marriage proposal until he was king of all Norway, inspired this vow.

The Unification of Norway

- Harald's campaign culminated in the Battle of Hafrsfjord around 872 AD, where he defeated rival chieftains and local kings.
- After this victory, he became the first king to rule over a unified Norway, though some enemies fled to Iceland and other lands.

Reign and Consolidation

- Spent his reign solidifying power, quelling uprisings, and establishing centralized rule.
- Implemented policies including land grants to loyal followers and taxes on coastal regions to maintain control and fund governance.

Marriages and Children

- Had several wives and numerous children, including sons who later fought for dominance.
- Notable sons include Eric Bloodaxe, who succeeded him, and Haakon the Good, who ruled with a more conciliatory approach.

Later Life and Death

- Handed over responsibilities to Eric
  Bloodaxe as internal struggles and family
  feuds weakened the unity.
- Believed to have died around 932 AD,
  though some sources suggest he may have
  lived a few years longer.

Legacy

- Harald Fairhair's legacy as Norway's unifier
  made him a central figure in Norse history
  and legend.
- His efforts laid the foundation for the
  Norwegian kingdom, and his descendants
  played significant roles in regional history.
- His story is immortalized in the sagas,
  blending historical events with myth.

Introduction to Harald

Harald Fairhair, also known as Harald I of Norway, stands as a towering figure in the history of Scandinavia, often celebrated as the first king to unify Norway. His life, rich with both historical significance and legendary embellishments, played a pivotal role in shaping the early Norwegian kingdom during the late 9th and early 10th centuries. The blending of historical facts and myth surrounding his reign offers a fascinating glimpse into the early medieval period of Northern Europe.

Born around 850 AD, Harald was the son of Halfdan the Black, a local king who ruled over a region in southeastern Norway. Harald's early life was marked by the fragmented nature of Norse politics, with the land divided into numerous petty kingdoms, each ruled by its own chieftain or king. The death of his father set Harald on a path of ambition and conquest. Upon inheriting his father's realm as a young man, Harald recognized the disunity among the various kingdoms as both a challenge and an opportunity.

Harald's quest for unification is steeped in legend, most notably the tale of his vow to not cut his hair until he had brought all of Norway under his rule. This vow, which would become a symbol of his dedication and determination, earned him the moniker "Fairhair" (Harald Hårfagre). According to legend, Harald's pursuit of a woman named Gyda, who initially refused his marriage proposal until he had achieved his goal of unification, inspired this vow. The tale of Harald's uncut hair, growing wild and unkempt, became a powerful symbol of his resolve and the arduous path he tread in his quest to consolidate power.

The historical reality of Harald's campaign to unify Norway began to take shape with his victory at the Battle of Hafrsfjord around 872 AD. This decisive battle was fought against a coalition of rival chieftains and local kings who had resisted Harald's ambitions. The defeat of this coalition marked a turning point in the struggle for dominance over Norway, and Harald emerged as the first king to rule over a unified realm. This achievement, however, did not come without challenges. Some of his adversaries fled to other lands, such as Iceland, carrying with them the Norse culture and influence, and leaving Harald to consolidate his newfound authority.

The period following Harald's victory was characterized by a concerted effort to solidify his control over the newly unified kingdom. His reign involved not only the suppression of uprisings and the management of internal dissent but also the establishment of a more centralized form of governance. Harald implemented policies that included granting land to loyal followers and imposing taxes on coastal regions, both of which were crucial for maintaining his authority and financing his rule. These measures were instrumental in transforming Norway from a land of fragmented chieftaincies into a more cohesive and organized kingdom.

Harald's personal life was marked by multiple marriages and numerous children, many of whom would later play significant roles in the kingdom's history. Among his offspring were Eric Bloodaxe and Haakon the Good, both of whom would go on to make their own marks on Norwegian history. Eric Bloodaxe, known for his own ambitious pursuits, succeeded Harald as king but faced considerable internal and external challenges. Haakon the Good, on the other hand, ruled with a more conciliatory approach, seeking to build on his father's legacy while navigating the complex political landscape of the time.

In his later years, Harald began to delegate more responsibilities to his son Eric as internal conflicts and family feuds started to erode the unity he had worked so hard to establish. The transition of power was a delicate process, and Harald's influence remained a crucial factor in guiding the kingdom through these turbulent times. He is believed to have died around 932 AD, though some historical sources suggest he may have lived slightly longer. His passing marked the end of an era of pioneering efforts to forge a unified Norwegian state.

Harald Fairhair's legacy is a compelling mix of historical achievement and mythological grandeur. His efforts to unify Norway laid the groundwork for the development of a cohesive and enduring kingdom. The sagas and historical accounts of his life blend real events with legendary elements, creating a rich tapestry that continues to captivate the imagination. The story of Harald Fairhair, as both a historical figure and a legendary hero, remains an integral part of Norwegian heritage and a symbol of the kingdom's early formation.

Early Life and Rise to Power

Harald Fairhair was born around the year 850 AD to Halfdan the Black, a prominent figure in Scandinavian history. Halfdan was a notable chieftain who ruled over a significant portion of southeastern Norway. His reign was marked by both military prowess and political maneuvering, laying the groundwork for the future unification of Norway.

Halfdan the Black was a descendant of a lineage of local rulers who governed various parts of what is now Norway. His control over southeastern Norway was established through a combination of conquest and alliances with other regional leaders. His rule was characterized by efforts to consolidate power and expand his influence, setting the stage for the eventual rise of his son, Harald.

Harald's early life was shaped by his father's reign, which provided him with both the resources and the political acumen necessary for his future endeavors. Upon Halfdan's death, which occurred around 860 AD, Harald inherited his father's realm.

The circumstances of Halfdan's death are not entirely clear from historical records, but it is believed that he died a natural death or possibly in a skirmish, as was common among rulers of that era.

Following his father's death, Harald faced the monumental task of managing and expanding the realm he had inherited. At this time, Norway was not a unified kingdom but rather a collection of fragmented petty kingdoms and chieftaincies, each with its own ruler. The land was divided by numerous regional rulers who often clashed with one another, leading to a fragmented and tumultuous political landscape.

Recognizing the need for greater unity and control, Harald embarked on an ambitious campaign to consolidate the disparate regions of Norway under his rule. This endeavor required not only military might but also strategic diplomacy and alliances. Harald's campaign to unite Norway was a prolonged and arduous process, marked by a series of battles and negotiations.

One of the most significant challenges Harald faced was overcoming the resistance of other local chieftains and kings who were reluctant to surrender their autonomy. Harald's efforts to subdue these rivals involved a combination of military confrontations and strategic alliances. His military campaigns were characterized by both decisive battles and sieges, aimed at bringing the various regions under a centralized authority.

Harald's rise to power was not instantaneous but the result of years of persistent effort and strategic maneuvering. His ability to unite the fragmented kingdoms of Norway was a testament to his leadership and determination. The unification process was marked by both victories and setbacks, with Harald navigating a complex web of regional loyalties and rivalries.

The campaign to unify Norway culminated in the famous Battle of Hafrsfjord, which took place around 872 AD. This battle was a pivotal moment in Harald's quest for unification, as it represented a decisive confrontation with a coalition of rival chieftains and local kings. The victory at Hafrsfjord was a turning point that solidified Harald's position as the first king of a unified Norway.

Following the battle, Harald continued to consolidate his power and integrate the newly acquired territories into a coherent kingdom. His reign was marked by efforts to establish a centralized administration and implement policies that would ensure the stability and cohesion of the realm. Harald's leadership during this period set the foundation for the future development of Norway as a unified and centralized kingdom.

Harald Fairhair's early life and the subsequent campaign to unify Norway were shaped by his inheritance of his father's realm and the fragmented political landscape of the time. Harald's efforts to bring together the various petty kingdoms and chieftaincies were marked by military campaigns and strategic alliances, ultimately culminating in the establishment of a unified Norwegian kingdom. His leadership and determination played a crucial role in shaping the history of Norway during the late 9th and early 10th centuries.

Legend of the Hair

The legend of Harald Fairhair, or Harald Hårfagre, is one of the most compelling narratives in Norse history, blending historical ambition with mythic symbolism. The tale of Harald's vow to not cut his hair until he had unified Norway is not only a testament to his determination but also a reflection of the deeply intertwined nature of Norse sagas and historical reality.

Harald Fairhair, born around 850 AD, was a prince of the Yngling dynasty, a lineage that held sway in southeastern Norway. His father, Halfdan the Black, ruled over a region fragmented into numerous petty kingdoms, each governed by its own local chieftain. Upon his father's death, Harald inherited this fragmented realm and faced the formidable challenge of unifying it under a single rule. The process of consolidation would require not only military prowess but also a symbolic gesture that could rally support and assert his claim to kingship.

According to legend, Harald's vow to refrain from cutting his hair until he had achieved this monumental task was more than a personal commitment; it was a powerful statement of his resolve. This vow was reportedly inspired by a significant personal and political motivation. At the heart of this vow was his pursuit of Gyda, a noblewoman of remarkable beauty and high status. The legend recounts that Harald, despite his growing power and military successes, was unable to secure Gyda's hand in marriage. Gyda's refusal was not a matter of mere personal preference but was rooted in the political landscape of the time. She allegedly declared that she would only consider marriage to Harald if he succeeded in unifying Norway.

This demand was more than a challenge; it was a test of Harald's ambition and ability. The saga suggests that Harald was deeply motivated by Gyda's refusal, viewing it as both an external validation of his quest and a personal challenge. The vow to leave his hair uncut became a visible symbol of his resolve to fulfill both his political and personal ambitions. His hair, growing longer and wilder with each passing year, became a tangible representation of his commitment to unifying Norway. The legend describes his hair as becoming a symbol of his unyielding spirit, and the longer it grew, the more it signified his unbroken pledge to achieve his goal.

The story of Harald's hair and his vow to remain unshorn until he unified the realm contributed significantly to his nickname, "Fairhair" or "Hårfagre" in Old Norse. The term, which means "beautiful hair," not only highlighted his physical appearance but also became emblematic of his extraordinary dedication and the grandeur of his achievements. It symbolized the idea that his commitment to unification was as enduring and noble as the flowing locks that he bore as a mark of his unfulfilled promise.

The unification of Norway, as chronicled in the sagas, was no simple feat. Harald embarked on a series of military campaigns against rival chieftains and regional rulers, consolidating power through both warfare and diplomacy. His victory at the Battle of Hafrsfjord around 872 AD marked a pivotal moment in his campaign, leading to his eventual establishment as the first king of a unified Norway. The length of Harald's hair, as per the legend, was not just a matter of personal choice but a reflection of the magnitude of his achievement. When he finally succeeded in unifying Norway, the completion of his vow was marked by the cutting of his hair, a symbolic act that was celebrated and remembered in the sagas.

In the historical and legendary accounts, Harald Fairhair's hair and his vow to leave it uncut until he had achieved his goal of unification became a lasting symbol of his leadership and ambition. The story highlights how personal determination and political goals were often intertwined in the sagas, offering a vivid portrayal of the values and expectations of Norse society. Harald's commitment, both to his quest and to his personal vow, reflects the broader themes of heroism and perseverance that are central to Norse sagas and legends.

unification of Norway

Harald Fairhair's campaign to unify Norway reached its dramatic climax around 872 AD with the pivotal Battle of Hafrsfjord. This battle stands as one of the defining moments in Norwegian history, marking the end of a long and arduous campaign to consolidate various petty kingdoms into a single realm.

Prior to the battle, Norway was a patchwork of small, autonomous territories, each ruled by its own chieftain or local king. These regions were often in conflict with one another, and alliances were fluid, shifting as quickly as the tides. Harald's ambition to bring these disparate lands under a single banner was driven by both personal ambition and a desire to impose order on a fractured land.

Harald's campaign began in earnest after he had inherited his father's domain. His early efforts focused on consolidating power within his own territory and then extending his influence over neighboring lands. He employed a combination of military prowess, strategic marriages, and political alliances to build a coalition strong enough to challenge the numerous regional leaders who opposed him. His campaign was characterized by a series of skirmishes and battles, each one bringing him closer to his goal of unification.

The Battle of Hafrsfjord itself was a significant and decisive confrontation. It took place in the fjord near present-day Stavanger, a location that would become synonymous with Harald's struggle for dominance. The battle was not only a test of military strength but also of strategic acumen and leadership. Harald faced a coalition of rival chieftains and local kings who had united against him in a desperate bid to preserve their autonomy.

The exact details of the battle are shrouded in the mists of legend and historical reconstruction, but it is known that Harald's forces were formidable and well-coordinated. His army, which had grown through the amalgamation of various factions loyal to his cause, engaged in fierce combat with the coalition forces. The clash was intense and bloody, with both sides fighting fiercely for their respective causes.

According to historical accounts and sagas, Harald's leadership during the battle was marked by extraordinary resolve and tactical ingenuity. He reportedly inspired his troops with a fierce determination, leading from the front and demonstrating both strategic and personal bravery. The battle was a grueling ordeal, but Harald's forces eventually emerged victorious. The defeat of the rival chieftains and kings marked a turning point in his campaign, solidifying his position as the most powerful ruler in Norway.

The aftermath of the battle was as significant as the confrontation itself. With his victory at Hafrsfjord, Harald effectively ended the era of fragmented regional rule and established himself as the first king of a unified Norway. The consolidation of power under Harald's rule was not immediate, as he still faced resistance from some regions and had to work to secure his control over the newly acquired territories.

Many of Harald's defeated adversaries fled the country to escape his growing dominance. Some sought refuge in Iceland, which at the time was a relatively unspoiled land, and others ventured to other distant territories. Their departure had lasting effects, spreading Norse culture and influence beyond the borders of Norway and contributing to the wider Norse diaspora.

Harald's victory at Hafrsfjord marked the beginning of a new era in Norwegian history. His reign, though not without its challenges and internal conflicts, laid the groundwork for a more centralized and cohesive kingdom. His ability to unite the various petty kingdoms under a single rule was a testament to his political and military skills, and it set the stage for the development of Norway as a unified nation.

The Battle of Hafrsfjord remains a symbol of Harald Fairhair's determination and vision. It represents the culmination of years of struggle and ambition, and it highlights the significant impact of his leadership on the course of Norwegian history. The unification of Norway under Harald's rule was a monumental achievement, reshaping the political landscape of the region and setting the stage for future developments in Norwegian and Scandinavian history.

Reign and Consolidation

After Harald Fairhair's decisive victory at the Battle of Hafrsfjord, he faced the immense challenge of consolidating his newfound power over a unified Norway. The unification of the disparate petty kingdoms was only the beginning; the real task lay in transforming a land previously divided by regional rulers into a coherent, centralized kingdom. Harald's reign was marked by a series of strategic moves designed to secure his control, quell uprisings, and establish a stable, unified rule.

One of Harald's primary concerns was solidifying his authority over the newly unified territories. With various regions and local chieftains still holding significant power, the transition from a patchwork of independent realms to a singular kingdom required careful and calculated efforts. Harald understood that mere military conquest was insufficient for lasting control; he needed to ensure that the regions he had subdued were integrated into a cohesive administrative structure.

To achieve this, Harald implemented a series of policies aimed at centralizing governance and reinforcing his rule. One of his key strategies involved granting land to loyal followers. By distributing lands to his most trusted supporters, Harald not only secured their allegiance but also established a network of nobles who had a vested interest in maintaining and supporting his authority. This system of land grants helped to create a loyal base of power that was crucial for stabilizing his rule. These lands, often granted in regions that had previously resisted his control, became a means of consolidating his influence and embedding his loyalists into the local power structures.

In addition to land grants, Harald also introduced a system of taxation that targeted the coastal regions of his kingdom. The coastal areas, which were economically vital due to their strategic position for trade and defense, became a primary focus for his revenue-generating efforts. Harald imposed taxes on these regions as a means to fund his governance and maintain the infrastructure necessary for a unified kingdom. The revenue collected from these taxes was used to support the administrative apparatus of the state, including the construction and maintenance of fortifications, the provisioning of the royal fleet, and the administration of justice.

The implementation of these policies was not without challenges. Many of the regions that had been integrated into the kingdom were resistant to Harald's centralized control. Local chieftains, who had enjoyed considerable autonomy prior to the unification, were often reluctant to cede their power and accept the new system of governance. To address this resistance, Harald employed a combination of diplomatic and coercive measures. He sought to placate some of the local leaders by offering them positions of authority within the new administrative framework, thereby incorporating them into his system of governance. For those who remained obstinate, he relied on military force and political maneuvering to suppress dissent and enforce compliance.

Harald's efforts to centralize power were also reflected in his approach to law and order. As part of his broader strategy to consolidate his rule, he sought to establish a uniform legal system that would replace the disparate local laws and customs that had previously governed the various regions. This move was aimed at creating a more cohesive legal framework that could be uniformly applied across the kingdom. The introduction of such a system was a significant step towards ensuring that the rule of law was consistently enforced and that justice was administered fairly across the entire realm.

The impact of Harald's policies was profound. By distributing land to his loyal followers, he created a network of supporters who were invested in the stability and success of his reign. The taxation of coastal regions provided a steady stream of revenue that enabled him to fund his administration and maintain the infrastructure necessary for effective governance. The establishment of a uniform legal system helped to integrate the diverse regions of his kingdom into a cohesive whole.

Despite these successes, Harald's reign was not without its difficulties. The process of consolidation was ongoing, and maintaining control over a unified Norway required constant vigilance and adaptability. The resistance from local chieftains and the challenges of integrating various regions into a single administrative structure were continuous obstacles that Harald had to navigate throughout his reign.

Marriages and Children

Harald Fairhair's complex personal life, marked by multiple marriages and a large number of children, played a significant role in the historical and political landscape of early medieval Norway. His marriages and progeny were not merely a matter of family affairs but had far-reaching implications for the kingdom's stability and succession.

Harald's marital alliances were strategic, designed to consolidate his power and secure his dominance over the fragmented Norwegian territories. Each marriage brought new alliances and helped to solidify Harald's control over different regions. His most notable marriages included his union with Åsa, the daughter of the king of the Hordaland region, and his later marriage to the Swedish princess, Ragnhild, which helped to strengthen ties with neighboring territories.

Through these marriages, Harald fathered a considerable number of children. His progeny were central to the continuation of his legacy and played key roles in the kingdom's subsequent history. The vast number of children, particularly his sons, became prominent figures in the power struggles that ensued after Harald's death.

One of Harald's most famous sons was Eric Bloodaxe, who succeeded his father as king. Eric, whose name evokes a sense of fierce and unyielding strength, was known for his warrior prowess and his attempts to assert his authority over Norway. His reign was marked by continued efforts to consolidate power, but also by significant challenges. Eric faced considerable opposition and struggled to maintain the unity that his father had achieved. His rule was characterized by brutal measures and political instability, which led to his eventual downfall and the loss of his grip on power.

In contrast to Eric's turbulent reign, another of Harald's sons, Haakon the Good, is remembered for his more conciliatory and reformative approach to governance. Haakon was known for his efforts to integrate and pacify the diverse factions within the kingdom. His reign was marked by attempts to foster unity and promote Christianity, which were seen as progressive steps toward modernizing and stabilizing Norway. Haakon's approach to leadership was more diplomatic compared to his siblings, reflecting a different aspect of Harald's legacy.

Haakon's rule, although not without its challenges, was characterized by efforts to build a more cohesive and less contentious realm. His policies and reforms were aimed at healing the divisions that had plagued Norway during and after Harald's reign. This more inclusive and conciliatory approach helped to establish a period of relative peace and allowed for the consolidation of the kingdom's achievements.

The differing paths taken by Harald's sons after his death underscore the complexities of his family dynamics and the challenges of succession. The struggles for dominance and the varying approaches to leadership among his children illustrate the difficulties of maintaining a unified kingdom in the face of internal rivalries and external pressures.

Harald Fairhair's legacy was deeply intertwined with his offspring, and their actions shaped the course of Norwegian history long after his death. The dramatic contrasts between Eric Bloodaxe's tumultuous reign and Haakon the Good's reformative efforts highlight the impact of familial relationships and succession issues on the stability and development of the kingdom. Harald's marriages and children were central to the narrative of Norway's early history, illustrating how personal and political dimensions were intricately linked in shaping the fate of a nation.

Later Family Life and Death

As Harald Fairhair's reign progressed, the consolidation of Norway into a single kingdom, achieved through his relentless campaigns and strategic prowess, began to show signs of strain. The internal struggles and family feuds that emerged threatened the stability he had worked so diligently to establish. The once formidable unity of the kingdom was now being challenged by the very forces that had once been subdued under his rule.

By the early 930s, Harald found himself increasingly burdened by the complexities of maintaining control over his expansive realm. The internal strife was fueled by ongoing disputes among the various chieftains and factions within Norway. The ambitious and assertive nature of these regional leaders, combined with the growing discontent among the populace, created a climate of unrest that Harald struggled to manage. His ability to maintain the same level of control and influence that had characterized the earlier years of his reign was diminishing.

The family feuds also played a significant role in eroding the unity of Harald's kingdom. The competition for power among Harald's own children, each of whom sought to assert their own claims to influence and authority, added another layer of complexity to an already tumultuous situation. The internal divisions among his sons and their rivalries with each other created further instability, undermining the cohesion that Harald had fought so hard to achieve.

In response to these mounting challenges, Harald began to make strategic adjustments to his governance. Recognizing that he could no longer effectively manage the kingdom's affairs on his own, he decided to delegate more responsibilities to his eldest son, Eric Bloodaxe. Eric, known for his own military prowess and leadership abilities, was given a significant role in managing the kingdom's affairs and addressing the growing internal conflicts.

The transition of power to Eric Bloodaxe marked a significant turning point in Harald's reign. Eric's appointment was intended to alleviate some of the pressures on Harald and provide a more dynamic approach to the management of the kingdom. However, the delegation of authority did not entirely resolve the issues that plagued the realm. The internal struggles and family disputes continued to simmer, and the kingdom remained susceptible to the challenges that had been exacerbated by Harald's declining ability to maintain direct control.

As Harald handed over more of his responsibilities to Eric, he began to withdraw from the public eye, spending more time in relative seclusion. His later years were marked by a gradual retreat from the demands of active leadership. The once vigorous and commanding presence of the king became less visible as he focused on ensuring that the transition to Eric's leadership was as smooth as possible.

Harald Fairhair's death is believed to have occurred around 932 AD, though historical sources provide some variation in the exact timing. The accounts of his passing reflect a period of both historical uncertainty and mythological embellishment. While some sources suggest that Harald may have lived a few years longer, the precise details of his final years remain shrouded in a mix of historical fact and legend.

The passing of Harald Fairhair marked the end of an era in Norwegian history. His legacy as the unifier of Norway endured, and his efforts to establish a centralized kingdom laid the groundwork for the future development of the nation. Despite the challenges and internal struggles that characterized the latter part of his reign, Harald's achievements in bringing together the fragmented petty kingdoms of Norway were a testament to his vision and determination.

The transition of power to Eric Bloodaxe and the subsequent management of the kingdom by his descendants reflected the evolving nature of Norwegian politics and governance. The internal conflicts and family feuds that emerged in the wake of Harald's reign were indicative of the complex dynamics that would continue to shape the history of Norway in the years to come. The story of Harald Fairhair, with its blend of historical significance and legendary elements, remains a key chapter in the rich tapestry of Norse history.

Harald's Legacy

Harald Fairhair, a towering figure in Norse history, is renowned as the unifier of Norway, a monumental accomplishment that shaped the destiny of the Scandinavian region. His legacy, which straddles the line between historical fact and myth, marks him as a central character in the annals of Norse legend. Born around 850 AD as Harald I of Norway, he emerged from the relative obscurity of a local king's son to become a symbol of national unity and strength.

The legacy of Harald Fairhair is inextricably linked to his dramatic and successful efforts to consolidate Norway's fragmented petty kingdoms into a single, unified realm. Prior to Harald's rise, Norway was a mosaic of independent territories, each ruled by its own chieftain or local king. This fragmentation not only impeded the political cohesion of the land but also made it vulnerable to external threats and internal conflicts. Harald's ambition was to bring these disparate regions under a single rule, an endeavor that demanded both military prowess and diplomatic acumen.

Harald's journey toward unification began in earnest after he inherited the domain of his father,

Halfdan the Black, who ruled over a small, yet strategically significant, territory in southeastern Norway. Young and determined, Harald embarked on a series of campaigns aimed at subduing rival chieftains and local rulers. His strategic vision and military skill were evident in several key battles, most notably the Battle of Hafrsfjord around 872 AD. This crucial confrontation resulted in a decisive victory for Harald, laying the groundwork for his dominance over Norway.

The Battle of Hafrsfjord is a pivotal moment in Harald's quest for unification, marking the beginning of his reign over a consolidated Norwegian realm. His victory not only defeated a coalition of rival leaders but also established him as the foremost authority in Norway. Despite this success, Harald's rule was not uncontested. Some of his adversaries fled to neighboring lands, such as Iceland, where they carried with them the cultural and political influences of their homeland, thereby extending Norse culture and influence further afield.

Harald's reign was marked by a concerted effort to consolidate his power and solidify the newly unified kingdom. He implemented various administrative and political reforms to stabilize the realm, including the distribution of land to loyal followers and the imposition of taxes on coastal regions. These measures helped maintain control over his territory and provided the necessary resources to support his governance. Harald's policies not only ensured the stability of his rule but also facilitated the development of a more centralized and cohesive Norwegian kingdom.

Harald's personal life, particularly his marriages and children, played a significant role in his legacy. He had several wives and fathered numerous children, many of whom became influential figures in their own right. Among his sons, Eric Bloodaxe emerged as a notable successor, continuing his father's legacy of rule over Norway. Another son, Haakon the Good, would later become a king known for his more conciliatory approach, reflecting the evolving nature of Norwegian leadership.

The transition of power from Harald to his descendants marked both a continuation of his legacy and a period of adjustment as internal struggles and family feuds began to test the unity he had worked so hard to achieve. Harald's later years were characterized by a gradual shift of responsibilities to Eric Bloodaxe, a move that reflected the complexities of maintaining control over a growing kingdom.

Harald Fairhair's story, rich in both historical significance and legendary embellishments, has been immortalized in the sagas of Norse literature. These sagas blend historical events with myth, creating a narrative that reflects both the reality of Harald's achievements and the larger-than-life qualities attributed to him by later generations. Through these sagas, Harald is depicted not just as a historical figure but as a hero whose actions laid the foundation for the future of Norway.

The enduring impact of Harald Fairhair's legacy is evident in the way his story has been celebrated and remembered. His efforts to unify Norway and establish a strong, centralized kingdom set the stage for the future development of the nation. The realm he shaped would continue to evolve under the leadership of his descendants, who played significant roles in the broader context of Scandinavian history. Harald's legacy is a testament to the power of visionary leadership and the enduring influence of historical figures whose actions resonate through the ages.

Don't miss the next book in the Viking Saga series,

The Epic of Eirik Bloodaxe.

IF YOU'VE ENJOYED THIS BOOK,

Please consider leaving an honest review at your favorite online book retailer. It's like sending a cookie to the author without having to spend a penny.